Amalie Berlin lives with her family and her critters in Southern Ohio, and writes quirky and independent characters for Mills & Boon Medical Romance. She likes to buck expectations with unusual settings and situations, and believes humour can be used powerfully to illuminate the truth—especially when juxtaposed against intense emotions. Love is stronger and more satisfying when your partner can make you laugh through the times when you don't have the luxury of tears.

Also by Amalie Berlin

Dante's Shock Proposal
The Prince's Cinderella Bride

Christmas in Manhattan collection

Sleigh Ride with the Single Dad
by Alison Roberts
A Firefighter in Her Stocking
by Janice Lynn
The Spanish Duke's Holiday Proposal
by Robin Gianna
The Rescue Doc's Christmas Miracle

And look out for the next books
Christmas with the Best Man
by Susan Carlisle
Navy Doc on Her Christmas List
by Amy Ruttan
Available June 2018

Discover more at millsandboon.co.uk.

THE RESCUE DOC'S CHRISTMAS MIRACLE

AMALIE BERLIN

MILLS & BOON

First published in Great Britain 2017
by Mills & Boon, an imprint of HarperCollins*Publishers*
1 London Bridge Street, London, SE1 9GF

Large Print edition 2018

© 2017 Harlequin Books S.A.

Special thanks and acknowledgement are given to
Amalie Berlin for her contribution to
the Christmas in Manhattan series.

ISBN: 978-0-263-07272-3

33416826  MIX
Paper from
responsible sources
FSC® C007454

This book is produced from independently certified
FSC™ paper to ensure responsible forest management. For
more information visit www.harpercollins.co.uk/green.

Printed and bound in Great Britain
by CPI Group (UK) Ltd, Croydon, CR0 4YY

First, I must thank Dr Trish Connor from the bottom of my heart for her help figuring out what was wrong with Penny! I knew she had to have had a childhood illness, and had a list of boxes that illness had to tick to make the story work, but no idea what the illness could be. She listened to the list, rapidly spat out several options, and generally was a lifesaver. Without her directing me to juvenile dermatomyositis, which I'd never heard of, Penny might have never come alive to me as fully as she did. Massive thank-you to Dr Connor.

I must also shower love on Robin Gianna, sister-in-law to Dr Connor, who handled the conversation one day over lunch while I was panicking. :)

Finally, I'd like to thank Amy Ruttan, Annie O'Neil and Robin Gianna for the brainstorming and handholding it took to get this crazy book baby born. Love you, ladies!

PROLOGUE

WERE IT NOT for the strong shopping bags protecting her clanking purchases, Penelope Davenport would never have made the walk back to her darkened motel, if the brisk, sometimes sideways shuffle she'd been doing through the gusting wind and sheets of rain could be called a walk. Whatever it could be called, it was better than her flying had been today.

Deep in the pit of her belly, she still felt the plummeting sensation triggered two hours earlier when the early autumn storm she'd been trying to outrun had caught them despite her best efforts, and a microburst had tried to slam her flying ambulance into the ground.

She still didn't know why they hadn't crashed.

Altitude had been on her side. And the storm's sharp down-blast of wind had probably only caught them at the edge. Luck no doubt could be credited with making her jerk the stick in the correct direction, tilting them out of the wind to where she could level out and avoid killing them all.

The energy, a terrible need to just keep moving, had stayed with her too. If she stopped now, her bones might burst from her skin.

Yes, she'd kept Baby in the air.

Yes, she'd been given clearance to fly between storms.

And they'd gotten their patient to a Schenectady hospital for treatment, even if they'd had to divert an hour's flight north to do it.

But she still felt responsible for such a near miss. Not only had there been almost death, but her partner, Dr. Gabriel Jackson, couldn't even treat their patient at the new hospital, having no privileges there. On top of that, he got a ruined night *not* doing whatever he'd planned on doing, and he was stuck in a powerless motel without supplies.

Precisely how she'd ended up hiking to a strip mall during the height of a line of storm cells for stranded-at-a-lousy-motel-during-a-power-outage supplies.

Anything to make it better. For her. For him…

There had been attraction between them from the jump. A chemical thing that sometimes made them look too long, and sometimes required she remind herself what they were and should be to one another. Professional. Coworkers.

The first week they'd worked together had been peppered with awkwardness only eased when they actively treated a patient. In the confines of the chopper, even though it maintained a mild hospital-like antiseptic scent, she'd babbled her way to every destination because the act of talking helped her keep from thinking too much. To keep from noticing the light cologne he wore with its hints of ginger. To block out that vibrating awareness that filled up the spaces between them.

But with all the crazy bouncing around in her head, none of that would matter tonight. They were just going to hang out, eat some liquor store sausage and cheese sampler, drink wine, play cards, and talk. Him for once, rather than her filling up the space. He knew more about her than she did about him.

A blast of wind flattened her into the side of the motel just as she'd reached the awning-covered walk that should've gotten her out of the rain. Another ten or so doors, and she'd be inside, and safe, and she could roll up in the bedspread like a burrito to get warm.

Dying of pneumonia from how wet and cold she'd become after all that? Yeah, that'd suck. Gabriel would probably find the biggest horse pills with which to save her life, just to punish her for having gone out in a freaking *monsoon*.

He'd do it all while being sedate and so handsome it was like a big cosmic joke. Of *course* he would have to look like that—jaw that still looked like geometry even with the beard he kept short enough she wasn't sure it was technically a beard, or just some long, perfectly groomed stubble. The best-looking men were always the least attainable.

They'd never spoken about it, never made a move, but there had come to be an understanding between them. Conversations that began with proclamations of the benefit of having such a great partner to work with didn't need many lines to read between. The way he would sit away from her during work meetings, always on the other side of the conference table. She knew what interest looked like in a man's eyes, and she'd seen it there, so his distancing techniques said everything else.

Just as she reached his room, she felt the bag with the wine start to tear, and captured the bottle with her thigh against the hollow metal door. Knocking with her elbow was all she could manage.

"It's me!" A sudden clap of thunder drowned her out. Not exactly the entrance she'd planned. Then again, she hadn't really planned much beyond go to the store and make tonight better. In the back of her mind she held on to *have a great time* as her final objective, because it was at least statistically possible.

If he was moving in there, she couldn't hear anything over the rain.

"Hurry up, I think it's going to rain!" *Ha-ha.* See, she still had a sense of humor, before her untimely passing from hurricane-induced pneumonia.

Another blast of wind smacked her in the back and wrapped her completely saturated hair around her face. It stuck like a furry squid.

She opened her mouth to curse the door down—

if she had to dig out her own key for the room next door it was all over. But as she began considering the logistics of juggling her tearing bags, the door opened. Before he could say anything, before he could yell at her for this exercise in ridiculousness, she grabbed her slowly shredding bag of wine by the rip and darted inside, the rest of her loot in swinging bags presently cutting off her circulation at the elbows.

"You think it's going to rain?" he said, like he couldn't tell a joke when he heard one. Because his mood was apparently so foul he couldn't even picture a reason to be in a good one. "Are you nuts? You walked somewhere in this? You look like you just got pulled out of the Hudson."

Laughing a little, she swung the bags up onto his table. "It was only about half a mile. I think. I don't know. I'm better at judging distances from the air, less good at it from the ground. Though since I've only been flying a couple years and been on the ground the rest of my life, you'd think it'd be the opposite."

For a normal person, it probably would've been, but Penny had learned young to judge distance by how far she'd be able to walk or roll her wheelchair. It was more a can-I-make-it-that-far? measuring system than something with math and numbers. Being now able to easily walk a mile, or whatever, in the pounding rain was something to celebrate. Not that he needed to know all that. It certainly wouldn't help put him into a better mood. He might even start fussing over her health—like her family still did on occasion, even though she'd been in remission for years.

"Niagara Falls is coming off the roof." Even though Gabriel's words were complaints, his tone had taken on that sardonic lilt that let her know that even in the dark he was shaking his head and saying words he really didn't expect to mean anything to her. Might even be rolling his pretty brown eyes.

"Yep. But what was I going to do, call a cab to go the equivalent of a few blocks? Rain's not going to kill me." She hoped. But, goodness, she needed to warm up. Which…she didn't have a plan for. No spare clothes.

"Your teeth are chattering," he noted.

"I don't know how you can see anything in here, it's dark."

"I can hear them clacking."

She clamped her mouth shut to control the noise and finished piling her dripping bags on the table so she could dig out the candles she'd purchased. Candles meant fire, meant light, and especially some kind of *heat.*

"I know you're trying to be nice."

"I am," she chirped, felt her voice wobble with her involuntary jaw wobbling, still determined to give Dr. Grouchy a better evening than the universe had conjured for either of them. Finding the matches and grabbing one of the candles, she created fire. And light. "Saw a strip mall on the way here with one of those cheapo general-store places beside a liquor store."

Clack. Clackity. Clack. She gritted her teeth until her jaw tensed and felt more under control. She kept the rest of it short. "Got supplies. You could play along, pretend you're someone who doesn't hate f-fun. M-might s-surprise y-you."

The last several words stuttered out and she gave up trying to pretend. She was cold. During her brisk walk in the downpour she'd stayed more or less warm. Standing around made the chill seep into her, and life become decidedly less livable.

Outside the storm continued to rage, and when a gust blew against the side of the building, she looked over and noticed Gabriel was in his underwear.

Gabriel was in his underwear.

How had she missed that?

Putting the candle down, she smooshed her wet hair back from her face, where it was obviously obstructing her vision, and looked at him. Beneath his carefully zipped flight suit he'd been hiding *all that*?

Even as dark as the room was, she could see the definition of abs in his rich, brown skin. Wide, solid shoulders. Hip flexors. Good God, the man had chiseled hip flexors.

Which would be something she could spend time appreciating as soon as she got warm.

"Did you get something dry to wear in that?"

"Would be wet if I had. But I think you have the right idea."

She fumbled for her zipper, fingers suddenly stiff and wooly, and failed to sufficiently grab the tab to draw it down three times in succession. Her fingers just slid right off the end when she pulled. A mild sound of alarm was all it took to set him into motion, and suddenly he was in front of her, taking over.

Under any other circumstances, she might hesitate to strip down to her undies with the partner she'd been actively trying to ignore her attraction to, but him peeling the sodden, freezing material down her arms at least provided an excuse for the wash of goose-bumps she knew were as much to do with him undressing her as her looming hypothermia. When he knelt to help her with the boots, she put her hands on his shoulders, and immediately wanted to mash her whole body against his. The man was hot, in every sense of the word.

At least that fear that had been pitting through her was gone now. She wasn't feeling…all that hesitant anymore either. "How do you feel about underwear hugging? You, me, mashed together. You're giving off heat like a space heater and I really like that about you right now."

"I'm a normal temperature. You're just cold. It doesn't have to be freezing temperatures to get hypothermia. You know that."

Yes, she did.

Despite the irritation lingering in his voice, his touch was gentle. Large, strong hands cupped the back of each leg as he helped ease her clothing off.

Beneath her suit, she generally dressed for comfort. That meant white cotton bikinis and a snug strappy tank top. Being endowed with modest curves had advantages, one being the ability to skip confining undergarments, especially under such unstructured clothing as a flight suit.

She puffed as he stood back up and she had to clamp her arms to her sides to keep from flinging herself at him. "Yell at me later."

"I will. After you've had a shower and warmed up." And he sounded like he meant it.

Gabriel pulled her back sometimes, providing a special kind of stoicism that balanced her out. She was used to some measure of grumpiness when she did something he found dumb, but after the day they'd had the idea of him yelling at her made her stomach churn.

"Do you hate me?" The words erupted from her mouth before she could give them a proper spin around in her head, and even though she'd just told him to yell at her later.

"Hate you?" He shook her sodden flight suit out and draped it over the other chair, then looked back down at her, his still handsome scowl flickering in the light of the candle. "Why on earth would I hate you?"

"Because I almost crashed us. I couldn't… I couldn't outrun it. I thought… But then the wind…" She faltered around, and suddenly the words caught up with her emotions, and she knew she was crying by the hot rivers on her frigid cheeks.

"You did outrun it," he said, his voice gentle. One strong arm wrapped around her, propelling her toward the bathroom. "You got us here. It was supposed to go south of us. Everyone said so."

Everyone said so. She nodded, squeezing her eyes tightly shut to stop that horrifying leaking. But it wasn't enough. Several big, gulpy breaths later, she gave up and turned to fling her arms around his waist.

Everywhere their skin touched, she grew warmer. The firm wall of his chest under her cheek, the strong arms that immediately came around her wrapped her in heat.

She needed comfort, to know that her partner, a doctor who treated her—the only Davenport at Manhattan Mercy without the title—like an equal, still had faith in her.

"You won't be afraid to fly with me after this?"

Her underthings were wet, she realized as she felt his skin start to cool, or at least stop feeling quite so warm through the soaked material. She was getting him wet.

"I won't. We'll talk about that later, but right now you need to get in the shower," he said, his mouth against the crown of her head. "Who knows if the water will stay hot for long, and you've stopped shaking."

"It wasn't raining that hard when I left," she muttered. The colder she got, the less intelligent her foray into the blistering rain seemed. No matter how good her reasoning at the time.

You've stopped shaking. His words swam up to her as he wrapped his arms around her hips and lifted, then walked into the darkened bathroom to deposit her right in the tub.

People stopped shaking when they warmed up, or when they got too cold and their bodies gave up shaking to get warm.

He adjusted the water quickly, then stepped in with her, positioning her under the spray so that the almost too hot water hit the back of her neck, then her head, and once it had had a few seconds to cascade over her, he turned her by the shoulders so that her back came against his chest, and the water warmed up her front side.

She shivered again for a couple seconds, and then relaxed back against him, her head on his shoulder, and her hands seeking his on her hips to drag his arms back around her waist. Standing under the spray, in their underwear...

"This went a lot different in my head."

"Did you sing and dance your way through the rain in your head?"

"No, the rain didn't factor in. I just thought, get the wine, get some food, get candles, cards, munchies... Talk to Gabriel and give him a good night to make up for whatever you had planned at home."

"I had nothing planned." His mouth was at her ear, and the words should've taken the edge off somehow, but she found herself spinning to face him instead.

Probably her third dumb idea of the day, but, unlike the first two dumb ideas, she just didn't care.

It was dark, the candle left in the other room,

but as she pulled the tank top over her head she heard his breathing hitch. He couldn't see anything as with the lights out the small, interior bathroom was little more than a cave, even with the door open to a slightly less dark room beyond. But he felt her skin when she pressed forward. Lifting her arms and rising on tiptoe, she didn't stop, although she satisfied that urge to mash herself against him, and still didn't stop when his head dipped to meet her kiss.

CHAPTER ONE

Two months later...

LOCKED IN A stall in the ladies' room at Manhattan Mercy, Penny leaned against the polished metal separating wall and stared at her watch.

Across from her, perched atop the toilet-paper dispenser, sat a white plastic wand that could change her footloose existence forever.

It seemed emotionally safer to watch the hand on her watch ticking by than to stare at the tiny display for the entire minute it would take for the one line to appear, or two—results on the test she'd put off taking for three weeks.

At first, she'd been unable to accept it was necessary. She'd had condoms. They'd used condoms. They hadn't even been purchased at the cheapo general store, they had just been in her bag in case some kind of life opportunity happened. It was New York City. She could conceivably run into anyone. Like that guy from that movie…the one with the smoldering eyes. And maybe he'd be drunk, bored, or somehow seduced by her ability to walk and chew gum at the same time, and then…*magic would happen.* If she had condoms.

A week later, she'd accepted they may have been old condoms.

Last week she'd known for sure she needed to take a test. It had *really* only taken a week or so to take it…

Still, hoping it was negative felt *wrong.* Because what if it wasn't? She'd already be in the running for Mother of the Year from procrastinating on a pregnancy test without making *disappointment* the first emotion she felt for a tiny life she'd created.

Definitely the sort of thoughts you never ever tell your child. Or anyone else.

Or even better, thoughts to avoid having altogether.

Every second the tiny hand ticked, her stomach grew heavier and more rumbly. When it finally passed the sixty-second mark, she lowered her wrist but still couldn't bring herself to look at the test.

This was not how women took pregnancy tests in commercials. They had pink bathrooms and a partner waiting outside the door, ready to celebrate, with something bubbly but nonalcoholic.

Which she didn't want anyway.

It would be all right. Everything would be all right. Nothing bad would happen just because she looked at the little window...

She closed her eyes and took a deep breath, shoring up her flagging courage that came with a twinge of self-disgust. The fact she even needed to boost her bravery should shame her into looking. Courage was a cornerstone of her entire personality. If something scared her, Penny had a personal maxim to run toward the thing, unless it was a bear.

Another deep breath slowly exhaled didn't help either.

Nope.

A minute—or even two now—wasn't sufficient time for this. Why didn't they make *delayed* response pregnancy tests so you could work up to it? It wouldn't have to take that long for the testing, just some kind of delay on the display.

I feel I'll be ready to look at this Thursday. Push the Thursday button. Then take that many days to come up with a plan for how not to freak out.

She couldn't wait for Thursday. She also couldn't look at the thing in a bathroom stall. Leaving aside questions about her emotional maturity, if she wanted to get in the pre-flight and maintenance checks before their shift started, she needed to go now.

She snatched the little wand and stuffed it into the thigh pocket on her flight suit, zipped that pocket closed, and barreled out of the stall to clean up and get upstairs.

The whole not-looking business was even dumber than her hike through a hurricane. She didn't need to look, the answer had burned into her frontal lobe before she'd swiped her debit card at the pharmacy. Regular Rosie didn't miss a single period, let alone two, for no reason. The test was a formality, therefore she was extra-stupid for not just looking at it.

Gabriel would've told her so too, only she'd

been unable to tell him about any of this before now. He would've picked her up, and squeezed her like an orange until she tinkled on the damned wand.

The morning after that night, which she still found herself lingering over in quiet moments, he'd suggested the things they'd done never leave the motel room. It became the No-Tell Motel, minus all the sleazy connotations, because he'd declared it and she'd agreed. It was the sensible thing. Gabriel never suggested things that weren't sensible, and sometimes he was the only reason she did things that *were* sensible. She'd seen the sense, despite not really wanting to see it.

When he'd opened the door to leave the room, she'd grabbed his head and kissed the breath out of both of them one last time so she could hold to that agreement. The hedonistic part of her, the part that loved life and experience, hated giving up that experience so quickly.

But? Sensible. She wasn't in the market for a relationship, at least not a *relationship* relationship, even if she could've carried on a little longer. Tried out other rooms and, through trial and arduous study, gathered the data to support the hypothesis their night had borne: sex with Gabriel Jackson was as good as it got.

But so was working with him.

She really had no idea what friendship would be like with him, or anything else outside work and the unspeakable night because, despite her efforts, they hadn't gotten to the cards and friendship-building conversations. They'd showered… vigorously. Then they'd made a mess of the bed even more vigorously. The wine had been drunk in between all that. There had been other pit-stops where they'd consumed cheese and sausage because stamina required fuel, but none of the business their mouths had gotten up to had been in the vicinity of talking.

Unless you counted *that* talk. The sexy smattering of words between lovers.

Just like that.

Don't stop.

Oh, God…

Heaven help her, she was doing it again. Thinking about all *that*, which had caused all *this*. The consequences.

She took the stairs at a run, pounding up the

ten flights separating her current floor and the helipad on the roof.

At the top, with blessedly buzzing lungs and legs, she checked her watch on her way to the chopper. Just over two minutes. She'd have to do better if she was going to make it up eighty-six floors at the Empire State Run-Up in the New Year. If she even could do the stair-climbing marathon while pregnant.

She climbed into the thing she'd been calling "Baby" for two years and worked through the checklist to go over gauges and start it up. Only when she'd finished did she sit back and reach into her thigh pocket to pull out the wand. Before giving herself a chance to think anything or to get worked up, she flipped it over and read the display.

Two lines.

Yep.

Out of the corner of her eye she saw movement. A full look tracked Gabriel's long stride eating up the distance between them.

"Dang it." She stuffed the wand back into the pocket and zipped it as fast as she could.

Then the door opened and he gave her a look.

"What?"

"Why aren't you starting it up already? Is there a problem?"

"What problem? There's no problem," she blurted, too fast and too loud, then gestured haplessly at nothing, trying to get back on course. "I've already done the checks. Why are you…?"

He never came up to the roof anymore unless they had a call.

"Did we get a call?" She looked at the radio and her stomach sank. *Off.* She hadn't turned it on during her pre-flight checks.

He said nothing, just turned the radio on while she started the massive rotors spinning.

"Where are we going?" she asked, buckling in, and by the time he'd answered she was ready to lift off. That was part of why she went through the pre-flight checks—it was set up to go from nothing to flight in under a minute.

"Is everything all right?" he asked through the comm once they were in the air. It wasn't concern she heard so much as that hint of frustration that appeared in his voice every time things didn't happen when he expected.

To lie, or not to lie…

"Can't complain."

She really couldn't, at least not right now. And complaining was something she tried to only do inside her head. Complaining about anything could still trigger her loved ones trying to rescue her, which she could appreciate on an intellectual level even if she couldn't abide it anymore. Complaining about anything related to health? That might even bring her whole family out in full flailing fit mode, maybe even with questions about whether she was healthy enough to gestate a human life.

The shape of the test in her thigh pocket stood out, and she prayed Dr. Notices Everything didn't notice until she was ready to share.

"You're pale. Are you sick?"

Gabriel might not understand much about what went on inside Penny's head but he understood her body unfortunately well, beyond just what his training had taught him about her physiological signs of distress.

Pale face and darkness under blue eyes so bright the blackness beneath them seemed blacker. Some kind of unsteadiness in her hands. The silent call radio. No music either during her pre-flight routine, and she always listened to music when on standby. Tight-lipped when normally talkative...

She squinted at him, then adjusted something amid the toggles and switches without answering him. Not right.

Despite the somewhat fumbling quality her hands had taken with switches, on the controls everything went smoothly. The flight was steady, a straight line, something he could appreciate since his life depended on it, but something was wrong. And if she stayed true to form, he was going to have to shake it out of her. Later. They were already in the air, so his chance to swap out a focused pilot had gone.

The two months since their...mistake...hadn't been entirely easy months. The first couple of weeks had been the worst. Awkward enough that she'd barely looked him in the eye any particular day, which had been rougher than he'd have thought. But with a little willpower, and a pact of mutual amnesia, they'd worked through it and things had found a new normal, somewhat off-center from the way things had been before.

Like when they bumped into one another changing in the locker room. She'd been wearing the same kind of simple and somehow ungodly sexy cotton things, and when she'd looked at him, he'd seen his thoughts reflected back at him. The pink that had infused every inch of her pale flesh had backed it up.

Not embarrassed. Aroused. And unhappily so. *Awkward.*

Now he changed in the men's room and avoided the locker room unless he had to, or unless she'd gone home for the day. His initial plan had just been to keep everything as low-key and low-stress as he could so that *she* could forget. He knew he couldn't forget, but he wasn't as prone to impetuousness as she was—he could resist. When he found himself watching the way she tapped the end of her pen on her lower lip while filling out paperwork, he could shake himself out of it. Stop thinking about her mouth. Not give in to temptation. But that seemed harder for Penny to do, so he just tried to keep temptation from coming up.

It had worked at first when they'd started working together and just had to ignore a spark, and it had even worked briefly in the middle of the time since their night, but a couple of weeks ago things had started getting tense again. Made no sense, and he didn't know what to do about it. Time was supposed to take care of things like this, but their agreement not to discuss it meant he couldn't even act as he would've in the past. Ask her what was wrong. Offer her an ear for her troubles. Just suss out symptoms and determine whether her oddness was physical or emotional... No easy course of action.

If this was attached to the desire for another night, he couldn't blame her, even if he *would* turn her down.

"How long?" he asked through the comm, since he already had one patient to focus on, righting his thoughts. If she wanted his help, she'd ask for it.

Normally he wouldn't have to ask how long. Normally his chattering partner freely gave information during flight.

She still didn't look at him, but she did let go of the controls with one hand to point. "There. We're landing on the roof next door."

Taciturn. Definitely something wrong. If he

didn't expect to need her paramedic skills, he'd put her on light duty for this run. But the patient they were flying to was a steel worker who'd fallen from the beams of a new construction site. Since they'd called for an ambulance rather than a coroner, all he knew for sure was that he'd need her at her best.

"We're bypassing stretcher. I don't know what the site looks like, the board is the only safe bet. Are you well enough to carry it?"

She did look at him then, her eyes narrowing to slits. "I can do my job. I'm fine."

Gabriel didn't argue with her, but he'd never heard the words "I'm fine" and had it be anything near fine. Even if she put up a fight to stay on the job anytime she was ill, she'd never looked so put out with *him* over asking.

With an easy touch, she put the chopper down atop the neighboring building, and he unstrapped and went to grab bags.

"Get the board," he ordered, wrenching open the sliding door and hopping out to make a run for the roof access door.

It always took her a moment longer to disembark due to having to power down the chopper.

Him running ahead to the patient was part of their usual routine as every second mattered and he did whatever he could as she brought up the rear.

He hit the stairs running, and took all eighteen stories down on foot. Waiting for the elevator always slowed them down.

Across the lobby with a nod to Security, he bustled out the door and rounded the building. Just as he reached the construction site, the manager met him, slapped a hard hat onto his head and led the way across the dirt and gravel lot, around piles of construction material, to the concrete pad beneath steel beams, and his patient.

No blood haloing his head, a good sign and something he'd seen enough on the job with jumpers and falls from great height. Heads didn't stand up well to concrete, unless they didn't hit first. The man had landed on his feet, at least briefly, and his head had probably hit last.

Gabriel fell to the man's side.

Unconscious.

Breathing fast.

He felt for a pulse, found a rapid rate to go with the breathing.

"How long ago was it?" He began gathering information as he fished out a penlight to check pupils. One responsive, the other fixed.

"Less than ten minutes."

"How far did he fall?" Gabriel looked up again at the open beams for one that would align with the man's location.

"About thirty feet. That beam there."

Onto concrete.

When he lowered his eyes again, he saw Penny running full tilt across the construction site—without a hard hat but with the backboard held over her head. That would help a little if someone dropped something on her.

"Get her a hat," he said to the manager, then went back to his patient.

When she reached him, she put the board down alongside the patient and then began digging into his bag to help, extracting a neck brace first thing. A hat made it to her head, but didn't slow her down.

"How's he doing? What's his name?"

He hadn't asked.

"Frank," someone answered, and Penny thanked him, then started talking to Unconscious Frank as she fitted the brace around his neck, explaining what she was doing, as was proper.

"He's seen better days. There's some kind of cranial hemorrhage or swelling, one pupil unresponsive. And I think internal bleeding, his heart is going hard. Get a line in him, saline."

He ordered, she complied. That was the one thing unchanged since their unfortunate encounter—she always worked hard and fast. Competent, and something more. She may have been born to society, but she'd managed to become compassionate in a hands-on way, and it made a difference in the way she treated their patients. She might not be one hundred percent today, but she was still fighting for them.

A whole family of doctors, and she'd become a paramedic. He should ask her why sometime, but knowing her adrenaline junkie tendencies, paramedic fit. They were the first on the scene for the big emergencies.

Opening the man's shirt, he looked his belly and chest over, noted bruising on his left rib cage, then began to feel his belly for telltale signs of bleeding.

Like the turgid area on the left upper quadrant. "How's the line?"

She flushed the catheter she'd just inserted into the man's arm, nodded, and then hooked up a saline line to it. "We're good. I'm going to pin it to your suit. It's wide open, do you want it slower?"

"No, his spleen is ruptured, I don't know how badly. Run the drip wide open. We have to get him in the air." He lifted his head out of the way and Penny produced a massive safety pin from somewhere, and clipped the saline line to the shoulder of his suit.

It wasn't exactly the kind of protocol taught in medical training, but she'd done it before. Once they got to the chopper, she'd have to fly them to the hospital, and unclipping it from her own shoulder to free her to fly would slow them down. The first time she'd done it, he'd been surprised, but over their months, working together, her unusual methods had ceased to be strange. She always had a reason for the things she did, and he didn't doubt she had a reason to be so pale and stiff-lipped now. Which was what worried him.

"Get his legs," he ordered once the bag swung from his shoulder, and waited until she was there.

On the count of three they lifted, moved, and lowered their patient, then secured straps.

"You and you, help me carry him," he said to the manager and another strong-looking worker watching them. "Let my pilot run ahead and get the chopper running so we don't lose any time."

Penny waited until they'd started moving, then went to take his bag of supplies, swung it over her shoulder, and ran. She would push the button for the elevator and have Security hold it for them while she took the stairs. That was how she worked. She thought ahead, and he was grateful for that.

So, whatever was wrong, she was probably handling it. Maybe he should just let her handle it. The problem was, he had to be the one who forced her home when she *did* get ill, or would admit to being ill. It had become a happily infrequent part of his job description, but a part nevertheless.

By the time they'd reached the chopper, the blades were whirring. They got Frank loaded quickly and he put his headset on.

"They're already prepping an OR." Penny's voice came through the comm. "A surgical team's going to meet us at the roof to type him for transfusion."

"What did you report?" He locked himself into the jump seat over his patient, and while she flew he affixed leads for the portable heart monitor and checked again for pupil dilation.

"Internal bleeding, most likely splenic rupture, irregular pupil reaction, possibly some kind of spinal damage, and unconsciousness."

All that was the most she'd said to him all day.

"Okay." He called in another update, laying on the need for an MRI, then asked over the comm, "Why did you suggest spinal damage?"

"Skydiving. Landing jars badly."

Not his favorite answer, but not wrong either. Leave it to Penny to frame things in terms of extreme sports activities, that was like her. Answering with so few words on a subject she could chatter hours about usually? Again, not like her.

No matter how hard she'd hit the ground running today, something was definitely wrong.

As soon as they'd handed over their patient to the surgical team atop Manhattan Mercy, Gabriel took Penny's elbow to keep her from following the team inside. Not letting himself touch her had been another way to keep temptation at bay, and even this casual, platonic touch to her arm felt exasperatingly intimate to him. But it had a purpose.

She turned to look at him, her elbow held out from her body at an unnatural angle, her brows up in question. On top of the high building, the wind blew loudly enough that talking meant shouting, even with the helicopter blades silent. He jerked his head back toward the chopper.

"You want to go somewhere?" She was nearly shouting over the wind, eyeing his hand on her arm again. It wasn't as though he gripped her in anger, though he'd admit frustration at having to have this conversation again, and his grip wasn't strong enough to hurt. Sometimes he had to grab her to keep her from flitting away.

A quick shake of his head and he answered with one word. "Talk."

The flare of wariness in her blue eyes only firmed his resolve. He released her, went and opened the sliding side door, climbed in, and scooted to make room for her.

If he hadn't suspected anything before, the way

she looked at the sky, at her feet, and generally stalled for time would've given it all away.

She had to talk herself into speaking with him.

After about half a minute, she squared her shoulders and marched over to board the helicopter, nearly closing the door behind her. It was enough to dampen the wind and make this conversation less stressful than it would've been if it had to start from a position of yelling, but remained open enough for easy escape.

She perched on the edge of the seat, one hand staying on the door handle, and looked at him. "What do you want to talk about?"

So ready to fly.

"You know what I want to talk about. You shot me a nasty look, but you never actually answered me. Are you ill? Because you look like hell."

Blunt. Maybe a little too blunt, but if that was what it took to get through to her, so be it.

"I'm fine."

"Pale. Black circles. No motormouth. No music before flying. No band radio. You didn't even know we'd been called out. Want to revise your statement?"

"That was a mistake. Normal people do make mistakes sometimes!"

"Fine. If you want to stick to the Not Sick story, then are you hungover? Are you distracted by whatever last night's festivities were?"

"Oh. My. God. You're jealous? That's what this is?"

She couldn't have shocked him more if she'd just decked him.

They'd made an agreement! And the only way to keep up his end was to refuse to rise to the bait.

"I have plans to be alive tomorrow. A distracted pilot is a bad pilot."

"Did I fly badly?" Her voice rose, bringing it right back to near shouting level. "Did I perform badly today?"

"No."

"No. I did my job just fine."

"You're distracted, at the very least, and you're a distraction. Whether or not you're willing to admit it. I can't focus on the patients if I'm constantly checking on you to make sure you're still upright."

"I'm not sick—"

"I don't care." He cut her off. "Do whatever it

is you need to do to function at your usual level. Do shifts in Emergency until then, I don't want you on my crew. I'll get another pilot."

A fierce blush washed into her cheeks but didn't detract from her paleness. It actually amplified how very pale she was against that bright red contrast.

"I'm so glad that you don't care."

Still shouting...

"Since you don't care, and I know you don't because we're not friends, this is probably the *perfect* time to put your mind at ease. It's *not* an illness."

She never liked him questioning her over sickness, which had always bugged him, like he should feel guilty for being concerned about her or about their patients. But this was extreme, even for her. His neck prickled and he fought the urge to touch her again, but this time because he wanted the connection that was still there. But her reaction was so far outside the bounds of normal, he couldn't be certain it wouldn't make things worse.

She ripped open the sliding door, climbed out, then forced her hand into a pocket on her suit. In the next instant she had something in hand, but before he could identify it, the thing bounced off his left cheek and she slammed the door.

She'd *thrown* something at his face.

He didn't know whether to go after her or let her stomp off.

A glance down confirmed the thing had bounced out of his field of vision. With a sigh, he bent forward to look beneath the seats.

There was some stretching and, although he'd spotted it, to reach it he had to smash his face against the front seatback and feel blindly.

As soon as his fingers curled around the length of it, his stomach bottomed out.

He knew very few things that shape.

And only one that could be an answer to what wasn't an illness.

He straightened, pulling his hand from beneath the seat, and looked down as his heart beat louder and louder, like thundering rotors.

Positive.

CHAPTER TWO

No SOONER WAS Penny off the roof than she was jogging for the stairwell. A woman couldn't make an exit like that and then be easy to find…in the extremely unlikely chance that a real, flesh-and-blood man would behave like a movie hero and chase after her. Not that she wanted him to, she'd just bounced a pregnancy test off his face.

She hit the stairs two at a time to head for her supervisor's office. Gabriel had demanded she go home, and she'd take that advice. Not because she was underperforming, she wasn't, but she'd be lying if she pretended she wasn't distracted. She was. And she'd be lying to herself if she tried to pretend she wasn't tired. Emotionally tired or physically, she had no clue, but both should resolve with the same treatment: a nap.

However, there was one accusation she would cop to that had no bearing on the situation—she definitely was behaving differently than normal, and it was hard to be filled with supercharged optimism when you felt like you were in an uncontrollable spin without a fixed point on the horizon to guide you.

Once she'd begged off for the afternoon, she hurried out and summoned a cab. Earbuds and her streaming music service allowed her to shut down for the ride home. It wasn't until she opened the door into her own private space that guilt began to ooze from her chest. She could feel it rising off her like toxic vapor.

She should've told Gabriel more gently and she *really* shouldn't have thrown the test at his head. He hadn't deserved that. But he'd just hit that sore spot, maybe unknowingly, and her knees had jerked. In those few words he'd made her feel she was on the cusp of being rendered helpless again, like a wheelchair waited around the corner, crouched and sinister. Like any second she'd revert to being an observer in her own life.

The flight suit she always changed out of before coming home still hung on her, so she dropped her bag on the way to the stairs to her bedroom loft above to go change into something lounge-worthy, then headed back down to fling herself onto the sofa.

If it was already two months in, she'd have seven, or something, to go. She should make an appointment with a doctor she didn't share genetics with. But how long before she was shuffled off to the side just by virtue of being pregnant, regardless of how healthy she remained during her pregnancy? How long before they took her off the chopper and made her work every rotation on the floor in the emergency department?

How long before she was sidelined by her *baby*?

She stared into the open rafters above, sighing at herself. There was a worse emotion to attach to an innocent baby than disappointment. Resentment.

That word didn't apply yet, but she could see it on the horizon, a black monolith on her own internal skyline. Would that be better or worse than the emotion she couldn't even deny to herself: the fear that her child would be cripplingly sick just like she'd been, but not be one of the lucky twenty percent?

* * *

Darkness fell over the city before Gabriel's day ended. Manhattan was never truly dark, but during the holiday season it was even brighter than normal. Everywhere he looked he saw festive reminders of the holidays, glittering lights, red bows, and jingle bells. In front of Penny's Tribeca building, a leafless tree had been wrapped in tiny blue lights that transitioned to purple and pink. Even the tiniest branches glittered like crystal, but in a funky way that let the outside world know the eclectic apartments they'd find inside the converted factory.

He liked Christmas in a vague sort of way, mostly as a quiet Christmas Day with his parents, but the rest of the season left him flat.

The test felt like an anvil in his pocket, and had all day. From his flight suit to the street clothes he now wore, it had stayed with him. Even now, hours later, he didn't know how to feel about it any more than he could figure out how to get it out of his mind.

He'd had his shot at marriage and a family a decade ago, and had proved insufficient to the task of husband, so he'd never gotten to the father stage of family life. It had been planned—big family, lots of children—but he'd missed important steps somewhere along the way, and hadn't yet figured out where he'd gone wrong. Once marriage had been taken out of his future plans, so had the idea of being a father, one of the many reasons he'd always been meticulous about safe sex.

As he made his way across the lobby, the differences in their lives came into focus. Temperamentally mismatched. Historically mismatched. Socially mismatched. Financially mismatched. He did well, but by Davenport standards… If she decided to exclude him from his child's life, the attorneys she could hire could see it done.

Her name on the directory pointed him to the top floor. Penthouse, of course. Old wealth.

Which put his next move in a light that people would probably misconstrue, but he'd make it anyway. Even if he'd failed spectacularly as a husband the first time out, even if they were entirely different kinds of people. Marriage before the child came would increase the strength of his rights. He'd like to think he knew Penny well enough to rule out the likelihood she'd bar him from his child's life, but he wasn't willing to bet on it. Look at how wrong he'd gotten things with Nila.

If he and Penny could work things out, it would actually be a good thing. She might be impulsive, but she was also kind, and the days they didn't work together, he missed the optimism that rolled off her for most of the day. He could live with that being part of his daily life. They were extremely sexually compatible. If they could work out some kind of understanding about the rest of it, it could work, at least long enough to provide the kind of stable base their child deserved.

Once outside her door, he rang the bell, and she opened it so quickly she could've been just standing there, waiting for him. Except she was disheveled and had the soft look of sleep about her eyes, along with wearing some rumpled cotton pajamas.

As soon as the door stood fully open, she launched in.

"Gabriel, I am so sorry." The words came in a rush and her arms hitched halfway up her chest and back, like she was about to hug him, but wasn't sure he'd let her.

It was the opening he needed. He stepped
through the door, closed it and flipped one of
the locks before turning back to her.

The stricken look on her face had him reaching
for her cheek. It had been in him just to comfort
her, let her know he wasn't angry, let her know
that things had changed again, but the haunting
light of vulnerability in her eyes pulled him in.

Instantly, when his hand cupped her cheek, her
eyes fell closed and she tilted her head into the
touch, like she'd been just as worried about their
fight, like she needed comfort too. Mercy, he
wanted to kiss her. And he shouldn't, that would
be a jump too far, too soon.

Instead, he gave a little tug to bring her to him.
Her arms opened and slid around his ribs and he
let himself hold her in an easy, relaxed embrace,
his chin resting atop her head as she breathed out
so slowly and deeply that he knew she'd needed
it.

How do you feel about underwear hugging?

Her question from months before swam back
to him, bringing a grin with it. There was something about her that felt great in his arms. Maybe
it was her perfect height compared to his, and the

way his chin rested on her forehead when she tucked in close, and how he could feel the fan of her eyelashes on the side of his neck. Maybe it was the combination of her slender, feminine frame and the strength he felt in it, or the mop of soft, wavy hair and how, when even slightly ruffled, her delicate scent drifted out, calling to something in his chest.

He just knew he liked it. He liked it enough to force his way through the rest of the questions and worries he'd had all day. Start the conversation. Get it going. Keep things calm. That had been his mistake earlier when she'd grown frustrated and pelted him with a pregnancy test.

"Are you all right?"

"Are *you* all right?" she answered, without moving an inch, but alarm bells sounded in his head. Health conversations always set her off, even if this was entirely a health concern.

"You felt bad earlier." He squeezed her a little tighter as he spoke, a tool he'd never had the opportunity to use to calm down these conversations in the past, so who knew how well it'd work?

"I was shocked. Sort of. I didn't feel sick, I just felt, I don't know, unsettled? Kind of nervous?"

He simply nodded, still trying so hard to take it slowly. Not to rush ahead, not to demand answers, not to drag her off to the court house or frog march her to the altar.

So, today's symptoms weren't directly related to her pregnancy, not in a physical illness way. That was something. Her pale shakiness was shock. Okay.

Now for the question he'd been dreading. A sinking, hollow feeling in his stomach made him want to hold tighter, so he forced himself to relax his hold on her and lean back so she'd look up at him.

"Are you going to have it? I need to know what you're intending."

As soon as the words came out, she stepped back from him, fully back until no longer in arm's reach, her own arms drawing up like even her appendages couldn't be within his orbit.

He knew her well enough to know that she'd respond best to calm discussion, even if he could feel his hackles rising. He didn't want a repeat of their earlier confrontation.

Her eyebrows came together, her eyes went wider, pupils dilating to the point the black overwhelmed the usual vibrant blue. Mouth open, breathing faster… Fear. Fear responses. What did that mean?

Tension stole across his shoulders as well, but the emotional landmine between them sat there, both of them frozen, as if even a wrong flick of the eyes could set it off.

Was she afraid of his reaction when she answered, any reaction, or was there a *reason* to be afraid if she responded?

"Penny?"

"What do you want me to say? I don't know what answer you're looking for." She swallowed and her gaze skirted downward, but unfocused, as if searching her own mind for answers. Until the fuzziness lifted, and she focused on his hip.

He followed her gaze to his right front pocket, and the outline of the test there. Maybe it would get her moving again. Ducking his hand in, he withdrew the plastic wand and held it out to her. "I want you to tell me the truth. We made a life, I deserve to know whether or not it gets to come into this world."

Penny felt her throat close as he produced the test, and offered it to her. But it was his words that brought tears. "You want it? You're not trying to tell me you...?"

"I want it. God, of course I want it."

The rasp in his voice echoed the truth she saw in his deep brown eyes. There was even a reverence in the way he held the test out to her she hadn't noticed before. It didn't simply lie on his palm, his fingers curled loosely around it, he cradled it—this nothing piece of plastic.

Whatever else happened, she could count on that. He already loved this child, or at least the idea of it.

She laid her hand over the test and curled her fingers over his hand, then kept right on going until she'd folded her arm back and dragged his around her waist. Her other arm up over his shoulders, she pulled back into the hug she'd escaped when his words had curdled her insides.

"I thought I'd bungled it all up. That you were going to shout about it, or just...not, you know, because...we weren't..."

Words refused to come into any kind of order, but the feel of his other arm around her waist

helped. Made it better. Even after all the tor-
turous hours she'd spent this afternoon practicing the words to use for the Get Out of Jail Free
speech she'd been planning to offer. And which
she should still give him, even if she was in no
way ready to jump into that conversation with
both feet when just the merest whiff of discord
had almost made her lose her lunch on him moments ago.

"You know, this is all your fault," she half
teased instead, but kept her voice light so he'd
know she was mostly teasing. "If you hadn't
had that rule about not mentioning anything, I
could've given you some warning. Like, 'Hey,
things are amiss in Uterus Land.' That's part of
what I felt so guilty about. I had a little time to
work up to taking the test, but you've only had,
like...eight hours to get used to this."

"I'm not used to it yet."

"Me either."

"But you want it." He needed to hear it again,
and that was okay. That was something easy she
could give him.

"I want the baby." She confirmed that part easily enough, but a little rueful chuckle followed.

"I *don't* want to be pregnant. At all. I'm trying not to freak out about that part, but I want this child. Really."

The hug started to go past the point where it was probably getting weird for him so, no matter how good he felt, she still felt compelled to try and be sensible. A quick kiss to his cheek, and she stepped back again, snagging the test as she retreated to the sofa to sit.

"Because of work?" he asked, following the conversation, as well as her, to the sofa.

Because it seems too much like sickness.

"Because it seems very restrictive," she said instead, and found herself again looking at the test she'd had so much difficulty looking at earlier. "And uncomfortable. I guess. Plus, there's… you know, figuring things out. I don't even know how to start that conversation, like—"

"We should get married."

He said the words so quickly she had to mentally replay his words to even understand what he'd said. Then came a giggle, which promptly turned to real laughter at the absurdity of the idea. He was playing with her! Joking around! Everything was going to be all right.

"Right? Like that! Because, you know, people are going to ask. I don't know why, but they will. Things at work, I guess that could be weird for you with all the Davenports underfoot. But we should try to be sensible, right? Like—"

"We should get married."

The second time he said it, her laughter was more a confused burst of air. When she looked at him, it stopped cold.

No matter how serious he tended to be, his expression was usually relaxed. At least as long as people were listening to him, and obeying, that was the other one. He was great at his job because the man had a massive brain and cared about people, but also because he projected an aura of confidence and subtle dominance, so people usually did what he said. Except her when she disagreed with him. And sometimes just because she liked to mess with him. Briefly. Playfully.

Which she definitely didn't want to do right now. His narrowed eyes and tilted head gave off a light warning, and killed the relaxed, joking conversation she'd thought they'd been having.

"You're being serious? I thought you were just trying to make like…a tension breaker."

"How many proposals have you ever heard of that were made as a joke?"

"I don't know. I never—" Was she supposed to come up with instances where people fake-proposed as a joke? She didn't have any, but she could identify other jokes that were outlandish and had never happened in real life. "Some days you barely even *like* me. Are you saying you love me now?"

"I'm not saying that. I don't love you, but love isn't a requirement for a successful marriage."

"Yes, it is. Have you ever seen my parents together?"

He skipped her question, and doubled down on his argument, "It's not a requirement. Marriage requires mutual goals, mutual respect, values, and when you add to it a not inconsequential sexual compatibility, it's got all the ingredients. That's before we even consider the child, who deserves the best start we can give it."

"Gabe, the only part of that I agree with is the part about the child." Okay, that was a lie, she agreed with the sex part, but if he was ignoring whatever he wanted to, she could as well. "This baby deserves the very best life we can give it.

But the pressure of a home with two people who don't want to be married to one another is not that. This isn't 1960. You don't have to marry me because I'm pregnant."

"If this were 1960, that's not the way this would go between you and me, and you know that."

He'd gone and stiffened up again, and not only did she feel bad for having laughed, she felt bad about her own reaction. Her nerves, usually made of steel, weren't up to another fight today. She tried again. "We don't have to marry to be family to this baby. You're already the father, and I'm already the mother. Rings and empty vows aren't needed to validate biology."

He stood and paced around her coffee table, arms folding in such a way as to draw attention to his shoulders, and the way his long, elegant fingers flexed over his forearms.

Not what she should be paying attention to. She was supposed to be convincing him that it wasn't a good idea rather than just rejecting him, though how this conversation had circled around to marriage, she had no clue.

"I don't want to be married. You don't want

it either. You don't want a relationship—you made that very, very clear two months ago. People who don't want to be married have the *worst* marriages. That's a lot to put on kids." Which brought up his point that she didn't want to discuss, but which she now felt compelled to because her mouth had gotten ahead of her to plural it to more than one child. "You know that there would be more than one, because you're right… We have…not inconsequential sexual compatibility. So, you know, this is a bad idea."

For once in her life she didn't want to stand up—she was still tired from her nap—but the way he prowled around made her stand. She put the test on the table, then followed around to his side and promptly wrapped her arms around his shoulders again, over the arms still crossed over his chest.

His already stiff posture turned into granite. She was hugging living rock. What had happened to the relaxed, affectionate man who'd arrived not even half an hour ago?

She squeezed tighter, pulling him down just

enough that she could rest her chin on his shoulder and her cheek against the side of his neck.

His arms twitched, and then uncrossed. He placed his hands at her waist, but did not hug back.

"This is the worst hug in history. You did much better earlier. Remember those hugs? Before and after we got a little panicky? You're supposed to use your arms, not just your big ole man hands."

"Not feeling a lot like hugging."

"You feel like playing some crazy game of hopscotch where you have to hop in every square to get to the next," she said, stepping back again but taking his hands. It felt like tread-lightly territory. "But that square marked marriage is a fake-out. You didn't need to marry me to make me pregnant, that's already been established. Just like I can carry a child to term and push it out of my body without a wedding ring on my finger. You don't have to marry me to be a dad. To share custody of our child with me. We are modern, civilized people. We can make our own family, have like…a parental partnership where we can be friends—which, by the way, it would be good for you to deny you barely like me like you didn't do a minute ago when I gave you the opening to—because we're adults. You don't want an unhappy marriage hanging over this kid's head before she even gets a functioning brainstem."

"You want me to have shared custody?" He cut to that exact part of her speech, once again ignoring the rest.

"Of course I do. I want my baby to know his or her father, to have a real father in her life. You'll be a great dad."

"With paperwork to make it official."

He really thought she was going to screw him over here. He may have skipped the opportunity to reassure her that he liked her, but he *did* like her. Genuinely, not just as his work partner. But he didn't trust her.

She let go and stepped back, her attempts at comfort having served no purpose whatsoever. "With papers to make it official."

They hadn't become friends over sharing their life stories, and they hadn't become friends over this child—it was far too soon for that kind of friendship to manifest. They'd become friends over work, over mutual respect and trust *on the job*.

They had to figure out how to transform that work partnership to something arguably more important. If he needed paperwork to do that, she could give it to him. And hope trust followed because this suspicion of his made her chest hurt.

The next morning, Gabriel found himself loitering in the staffroom rather than going up to the chopper ahead of receiving a call. He had no reason to stay downstairs, he just needed some space. He had no power over her, outside the ability to send her home from work when she tried to soldier through sickness. He couldn't *make* her marry him, but couldn't make himself give up on the idea either.

He had a living example of the outcome to a kid disadvantaged in the parent department. Plenty of kids came through it fine, but he didn't want to take the risk. He wanted his child to have exactly what he'd had growing up: a mother and a father, both offering stability, love, an atmosphere to flourish in. It was in their power to provide that. Whatever she'd been on about with her parents, it couldn't have been that bad. All their children, except Penny, were doctors. She was successful in her own right, and worked every day to help save lives. She made some other questionable decisions, but nothing malignant.

He should probably go check on her, wade in early, but he just wasn't up to it yet. And she never hung out in the staffroom. Ever in motion, she was always doing something—checking inventory, restocking, performing routine checks on the equipment, or visiting with people in the department so she didn't have far to go when a call came. Her oddest and most recent habit had become running up and down the top three flights of stairs, something he'd taken every opportunity *not* to ask her about. Especially after that night, when he'd decided distance was the only way to get them back to professional-only interactions. Knowing more than she had already just randomly shared would make that harder. But now it was one of a million of questions he should ask.

Not asking had never helped anyway. He still had a bevy of inappropriate thoughts. That was before yesterday had forced their night back to the front and center of his thoughts.

His radio crackled and Dispatch blazed through, announcing their first call of the shift. Time to face the music.

When he reached the chopper, she already had it fired up, ready for him. Only when he climbed in, Penny wasn't at the pilot's controls. It was a man.

Lawson.

They'd flown together a couple times, and he was a competent pilot and paramedic, but he wasn't Penny.

"Where's Penny?"

"Don't know. They just called and asked me to come in and pick up her shift. I guess she's sick."

That sharp pinch at the back of his neck returned.

Sick and called off without a showdown? Was that some kind of carry-over from yesterday's battle, or was she really sick?

Grilling Lawson wouldn't get him answers, and they had a job to do: someone waited for their help. He buckled in and put on his headset. "Go."

Making the decision to focus didn't mean it was so easy to do so.

Penny was stubborn, perhaps the most stubborn person he'd ever met, so it was entirely possible she'd called off to make some kind of point. Last night had started out better than it had ended, but he'd thought the situation at least set to neutral when he'd gone home.

If she called off but didn't call him, did that mean anything? Could she have just called off to go to the doctor?

If she had called off on her own because she was ill, she must be *very* badly off.

"What's wrong, boss?" Lawson's voice cut through his thoughts.

He turned to look at the pilot. "Nothing. Why?"

"You just sighed massively. I didn't just come off shift or anything, I'm not going to be operating at some lower level today than any other shift. Chill."

Chill.

"I know. We're good," he said simply, no desire to engage in further conversation about it. It would be even more futile than the thoughts ricocheting around his cranium.

Whatever was wrong, she should've damned

well called to tell him. So much for all her talk last night of wanting him involved.

Soon enough, they arrived at their site and landed, and he had something else to occupy his thoughts.

CHAPTER THREE

So. Much. Vomiting.

Penny's cluttered coffee table practically sagged with barely touched beverages. And two buckets, along with the one she had on her lap. Because nothing stayed down.

It had started around three in the morning, rousing her from a dead sleep, and fifteen hours later showed no signs of letting up.

Electrolyte-enriched sports drinks couldn't help you stay hydrated if they didn't stay down.

Neither would the ones for children, which were honestly more gag-inducing.

Water wouldn't stay down.

Big *no* to milk. No to broth. Juices came straight from the devil. And she still had a crate of untouched other beverages she'd had delivered this morning, and which she'd try to pour down her gullet as soon as she'd got her nerve back up, along with the corresponding energy required to haul herself fifteen feet from her sofa to the kitchen island.

The one bright spot of her day had been not vomiting on the delivery boy. She may have tipped him enough to pay his rent—she couldn't be sure what she'd handed him at this point—but at least she knew he'd come back on future deliveries, rather than avoiding her apartment unless decked out in a hazmat suit.

She knew enough medicine to know dehydration was winking at her from just around the corner, but she didn't know at what point all this would become a danger to the baby.

The doorbell startled her as she reached for the tea she'd yet to sample, and the minuscule amount of fluid her body had been able to replenish in her stomach curdled.

Over her mostly dry heaving, she heard her name shouted through the door.

Oh, it was Gabriel. And he sounded like he was planning to beat the door down.

Would it be easier to let him and just get the door fixed later, or to crawl piteously on her belly across the floor so she could open it first?

As soon as she stopped heaving for a few seconds, she snatched a clean bucket from the table and slogged to the door. If nothing else, he could see what she looked like when *actually* sick, for future reference.

No sooner had she gotten the door open than a fresh round of heaving turned productive and she had to slump on the wall beside the door as she curled over her bucket, and mostly hit her target. Which was at least better than vomiting on Gabriel, the second lucky person she hadn't vomited on today, but who would've at least been less likely to hold it against her than the delivery boy.

"Good God, Pen. Why didn't you call me?" Gabriel ignored the anger that had percolated in him all day and stepped over the tiny puddle that had missed the bucket. Scooping up her, along with her bucket, he carried her to the sofa. Although slender, the boneless drape of her body made her feel even more insubstantial than usual.

He arranged her on the sofa, bucket cradled in her lap, and stood back to get a look at the loft. For perhaps the first time ever when accused of being sick, Penny didn't offer any lip or any resistance. By the look of her, talking might be too much. Every time she opened her mouth, retching sounds followed.

"Okay, maybe not called, but you could've texted." He relented, eyed the full glasses and mugs on her coffee table. "None of these wanted to stay down? Just nod or shake your head."

She shook her head.

Yesterday she'd been pale. Today she almost looked dead—all she was missing was that terrible shade of gray.

"Been going on all day?"

She nodded again.

If she'd looked this bad yesterday, he'd have dragged her into the ED and maybe had her admitted.

"Did it start before you woke up? Did it wake you?"

She nodded again, then did something so uncharacteristic, he felt for the third time in two days that the world had gone off its proper tilt. She started to cry.

"I'm not mad," he said in a rush. Even though he had been angry all day, seeing her like this made his anger feel like something entirely less righteous. And he still had absolutely zero idea how to deal with a crying partner. "Stop that."

Okay, maybe not the right thing to say. Should he hug her?

"It's okay. We can fix this. Just stop crying. I'll get some medication delivered. Concentrate on breathing. Everything's fine. Don't cry."

Fumbling his cell out, he dialed a friend in the hospital. By the time he got the medicine ordered and delivery scheduled, she'd stopped sniffling and started dry heaving again. Which…was a little easier on him, and which he'd feel guilty about later. After he also called a local grocery for ginger and a selection of teas.

"Gabe…"

He turned back to her, stepped over a bucket, and eased himself onto the couch beside her. "It'll be here soon, and will keep you from vomiting, even if it puts you to sleep. I don't work tomorrow. I'll stay. Everything will be okay."

One thing he made himself *not* say again: *Don't cry.* Even if it was right there in his mouth, bashing against his teeth to get out.

The look on her face was one of pure misery, but she nodded.

Seeing her state may have dissipated his irritation, but the frustration still hung around, especially when she weaseled her way under his arm and tucked in beside him so tight he knew she wasn't just physically miserable. She was scared.

"Hey…"

Don't cry...

She tilted her head back to look at him, and he found himself squeezing her a little tighter.

"Don't worry about any of this. I'll get it done. Don't worry about the baby either. It's still early to worry about this becoming a danger."

Her lower lip quivered, but she nodded again.

"Do you trust me to do what's best for you both?"

She nodded again, and the quiver settled down, her eyes becoming more focused, more certain.

"Then don't worry. Stress will just make things worse. It's early days to panic. I know that's easy to say when I'm not the one vomiting, but still true. I'll stick around until you're feeling better. Close your eyes and rest. I'll take care of it."

Still no argument. She couldn't get closer to him with clothes on, but it somehow made him feel better too, even if her slender frame felt fragile to him at that moment.

The antiemetic would help. And if it didn't, they'd visit the ED for IV fluids before dehydration became a massive issue.

"I know you're trying to be nice..." Penny said from the sofa the next morning, watching Gabriel scramble eggs in her kitchen, and alluding to the night they weren't supposed to ever mention, and which they still hadn't really spoken about, even after he'd slung sexual compatibility at her in that long, fraught conversation.

Gabriel dished the eggs onto one plate, but she knew he'd caught the words he'd said to her that night when he lifted his dark brown gaze to hers. She could almost see him silently working through whether or how to respond, and whether their mutual non-conversation treaty had any bearing.

"I'm not trying to be nice," he said finally, quietly, then followed it up with a redirect. "These eggs are for me. I already made you my mom's cinnamon apple tea, which I see is staying down."

Acknowledged, but not deepened. She had no

idea what that meant. Was the subject still forbidden? Should it be? She didn't want him getting back on that marriage thing, even if having him there the past day had been nice. Comforting, even. Which was annoying on another level but, still, she didn't want to say anything that made him stiffen up again, or start demanding legal documents.

"It is." She used the cinnamon stick like an inefficient straw to sip the cider and breakfast tea combination. "It's good. Really good. Remind me to send her a thank you for raising such a good man."

The sudden cocking of his head and the surprise she saw all over him surprised her in return. Was it so surprising that she'd say that? She mentally rewound through the past few days, then the past few weeks. When was the last time she'd said something nice to him?

She wasn't mean by nature, but she had to admit that the shock and fear of the past three weeks had perhaps, no, had definitely made her less pleasant than normal. Unless you counted beaning him in the face with a pregnancy test, then it probably had made her completely unpleasant. She just plain hadn't been herself, but if they were going to make this work out well for the three of them, she needed to find her way back to her much-preferred vigorous optimism.

"You're just saying that because I cleaned up so much vomit the past eighteen hours."

"I'm not," she said, then grinned. "I won't lie, that didn't hurt. A good man would do that for an ill friend, right? But, genuinely, it's nice that you're here. Comforting. I don't even really mind having you fuss over me, which is kind of a big deal for me."

"You're a little better today, so I've been expecting my marching papers since you've managed to stay awake for half an hour without trying to turn yourself inside out."

Still deflecting. Did she not sound sincere? Did he just really want to go? The latter thought brought a rush of disappointment that left her staring into her drink for several long seconds.

"If you want to go, I'll probably whine, but I won't stop you." As if she could. Her only superpower right now was regurgitation. "Do you not believe I want you here?"

While eating his eggs, he did the courteous

thing and stayed in the kitchen, eating at the snack bar on the rear side of the island—where proximity to eggs was less likely to make her sick. "I think you do now, but tomorrow will probably be a different story."

She took another sip of her non-alcoholic toddy. The context to her confession mattered, and he should know it. It had been years of work to put that behind her, and she did everything in her power to keep those two versions of herself from intersecting, especially with people she didn't want thinking less of her or diminishing her capabilities, but the introduction of a child changed that equation. He should know, and not just because it would make clear to him how much she appreciated his care. If their child developed the disease, he should know it was possible ahead of it coming to pass.

"What do you know about juvenile dermatomyositis?" She asked this quietly, but knew he'd heard her by the pause of his fork.

After a moment, he went with her direction change. "Rash. Muscle weakness. In adults. Juvenile? I think it starts pretty young. I'd have to refresh my memory for more information. Why do you ask?"

"I had it." She shifted on the sofa to sit up straighter, just to remind herself that she *could* move however she wanted to now. "Autoimmune disease, can be triggered by infection, or not. Usually treated with steroids, but sometimes they don't work and chemotherapy drugs are required."

As she spoke, a frown crept over his handsome face, and although she could still see a pile of eggs on his plate, he put his fork down and swiveled on his stool to look at her. "Do you still require treatment?"

"I'm one of the lucky twenty percent in full remission." She hated putting herself into those memories, because there was no distance. Even after a decade-plus years of remission, if she thought about it, she went right back there and all she felt was confinement. "But it ravaged me before they got it under control."

Ravaged was the only word she could think of to describe the effects and aftermath. Also, because she didn't talk about that part of her life. She'd shut it away behind thirty thousand feet of brick wall, and didn't even like her family to talk about it. That habit left her with a dearth of words to apply, she didn't even know how to start or if she even needed to describe it. She'd much rather gloss over those details, give him the lowlights, as highlights was a word she couldn't apply.

"How bad?"

"I was in a wheelchair for years," she said, because getting this word train going was hard. But it actually got a little easier as she kept on. "I had physical therapy every day from six to thirteen to keep my limbs from withering. If I couldn't get to the rehab center because of vacation or holiday, my parents put me through my paces. As doctors, they knew what could happen and wanted me to have the best shot at a normal body, even without knowing if I would ever recover to use it."

"You resented it?" he asked, but there wasn't any condemnation in his voice. He treated children so he knew how hard it was for them to cope with illness.

"Sometimes," she admitted. *"You're going to be one of the lucky ones*, they liked to say. I kind of resented that. Actually, I hated that. But they didn't give up, and didn't let me give up. I should probably thank them for it every time I see them, now that I fully understand I wasn't just in the midst of a caging illness but an illness that could've been fatal."

That wasn't all of it, that wasn't even the tip of the iceberg, but she could see him starting to put the pieces together. It was more to make him put the *right* pieces together that she kept going. "I'm healthy now, but I've been smothered by loving caretakers so much, I feel like I've used up my lifetime allotment of fuss."

"I had no idea." He abandoned his half-finished plate and came to sit right next to her, his thigh pressed to hers and his arm going immediately around her shoulders.

Would that simple touch from him always be able to push the tension right out of her? She closed her eyes, tried to make herself focus on all those words she'd said, all the reasons she shouldn't take the comfort he gave without hesitation.

"That's why you refuse to call off when you're ill?"

That wasn't one of the threads she'd hoped he'd

pick up on, but she nodded, then pressed closer still. "When I say I don't mind you taking care of me, you should know that's a position of dubious honor. I *really* appreciate you coming over to check on me, and staying. No joke. Thank you. I'm sorry I didn't call or text to tell you I was sick. It honestly never occurred to me, but I will. From now on."

His lips on her forehead brought a shock of need bubbling up inside her. Not for sex, though being close to him pretty much meant it was in the back of her mind all the time, but something like sweetness and sadness mixed together. Like homesickness.

"I know I'm weird and sometimes kind of wild in reaction to having spent years living my life on the sidelines, and I don't want that for my...for *our* child. She, or he, should just get to be whoever she would be without leagues of childhood trauma making her into someone who drives everyone bonkers." She felt his arm tighten, his lips still lingering on her skin, relaxed now, but no less sweet.

"You don't make me crazy." His lips feathered against her forehead.

"You're not selling that line in this house, Jackson." She leaned back, breaking the chest-aching touch to look him in the eye. "I could pass it on. I don't know how likely it is, or what it would take. I don't really know anything about the genetics of the disease, just that it is genetic."

"Did they find a cause for your dermatomyositis?"

"At the time they said it was idiopathic. In my adult life, I've done everything possible to not revisit it. I haven't kept up on the latest findings."

He made a sound she couldn't define, and reached over to retrieve her mug and press it back into her hands. Emergency physician, he had to deal with the problem currently on his plate, and her looming dehydration was it. "Drink half and I'll let you sleep. I know the medication makes it impossible to stay awake for long periods."

Another sip and she started to relax again, really feeling better than yesterday—well enough to push liquids a little more vigorously than sips. At least while she had a man with a mop watching over her.

"Will you check your medical journals to see what the latest research on JDM is, like the likelihood of passing it on? Does it require two carriers or one? None of my siblings have it."

"Drink."

She bypassed the cinna-straw and took a big apple-y pull.

"I'll read while you're asleep."

"And see if there's any genetic testing I should have?" Another big drink.

"Okay, drink slower." He urged the mug back down after her second big gulp. "You've finished half. You can stop if you want to."

She relented for the moment, at least on the drinking front. "The testing?"

"I'll see what I can find out. I can always call one of the pediatric specialists at Mercy if I need to."

Satisfied, she went back to the drink. "I think I can finish it."

"Don't make yourself sick, or we'll have to start all over."

"It tastes good."

He stopped arguing, but the softness in his eyes when he looked at her said he wasn't yet unconcerned. "Have you made an appointment with your OB?"

"No, but I only officially knew I needed to for two days, and yesterday I spent the whole day wondering if I should strap the bucket around my neck or install a headrest on the toilet seat."

That got a little smile from him, and then a little distance. He moved away and sat forward, as if preparing to flee. "Fair enough. Want me to do that while you're asleep?"

Then he was up, and she missed not only the heat of him but the comfort that had seeped into her from the brief cuddle, and especially from that utterly chaste kiss. She couldn't remember the last time anyone had kissed her head like that, like she was the sweetest thing in the world.

Which could've been a trick. It'd be a good one. *Marry me, I'm a forehead-kisser.* Not a bad line of argument, if she didn't have more than a decade of watching her parents implode to know how far from marriage she wanted to stay.

She mumbled the doctor's name and slid down into the nest she'd been living in on the couch since yesterday, when what she really wanted was to ask him to lie down with her. If she closed her eyes, she could still remember the way his strong, steady heart had thudded beneath her cheek when he'd held her as they'd come down from another sweaty tumble.

That wasn't the relationship they had now, though, so she tugged her blanket over her and didn't stop until it was snugged up to her chin, but the only warmth she felt was in the sofa cushions beneath her where he'd been sitting.

If she wanted more from him, things would get messy. This was probably just a reaction to their situation. She needed something, and he was in White Knight mode. Who knew how far that was from Husband mode?

As she settled, he took her mug and headed for the kitchen, cellphone already out to start making calls.

Probably hadn't even noticed her needy lapse in judgement. Which had to be good. It just didn't feel like it.

"Am I carrying you to bed or are you walking?" Gabriel asked, standing above the Penny-shaped lump burrowed under the blanket on the sofa. Somehow, he was again willing to forgo his rule never to sleep beside any of his lovers. A rule he'd only broken once since his divorce. With her, that night.

With the frown he saw marring her still-pale face, he knew he was testing the boundaries of her gladness at having him around, but after about thirty-six hours of very little sleep he was willing to push a little. That's what he told himself for the thirtieth time, that this was just practical. His decision had nothing to do with the little rush he felt when he considered it. That feeling was worry, not anticipation. Definitely not anticipation.

She rolled her head around dramatically and forward until she cupped one hand over her eyes. "I can sleep on the sofa. It's comfortable."

"But we can't both sleep on the sofa, and I don't want to sleep on the floor."

She squinted at him, starting to catch up. Since she'd downed the first antiemetic, she'd been sleeping so much she barely knew what time it was, let alone how many hours he'd spent hovering. "Did you sleep on the floor last night?"

"Dozed off and on in the chair." Had woken up every time she'd made a sound. And part of that was not wanting her to go through this alone, but another part of it was pure manipulation, something he wasn't sure how to think about. Penny wasn't his enemy, but she could become his enemy if she decided she didn't want him involved with their child after all. Keeping her close, where he could keep an eye on her and pay attention to make sure he spotted it if things suddenly began to go sideways, was the less humanitarian aspect.

"You could've slept in the guest room, still can. It's made up."

"I wouldn't hear you if you woke in distress if I was asleep in another room," he said, and then just confronted the issue. "Do you have a problem with me sleeping in the bed with you?"

"I'm just surprised…"

"Wouldn't be the first time," he reminded her gently.

She looked at him a beat too long. "I know, but are we talking about that now? Obviously, I'm not going to put the moves on you this time, if I put them on you last time. I'm not entirely sure if I did."

"You did."

"Which moves did I make?"

"You went and bought wine to get me drunk and take advantage of me in a seedy motel." The smile blooming on her face made him glad he'd gone with the joke, even if they shouldn't really be trying to make this more comfortable than he already knew it would be.

She picked up her bucket. "That's not how I remember it. But if you want to pretend I stole your virtue…"

It had been hours since she'd needed the bucket, but it obviously made her feel more secure, so he didn't say anything. Just double-checked the door was locked, and then followed her upstairs. "You were the one to suggest underwear hugging."

"I was freezing to death." She must be feeling better, she was arguing again. "I sleep on the right, which is good for bucket placement. I have nightmares of barfing on you."

"It's high on my list of hellish situations too." All he could think to do was revert back to their between-cases banter, treat everything as business as usual for now. And he kept telling himself that as she crawled into the bed and he stripped down to his boxers and T-shirt.

"If you're staying here in this bed because of obligation…"

"I'm staying because I want to be here. Do you prefer me going to the guest room? I can assure you nothing is going to happen." He sat on the edge of the bed, turned to regard her, and bit the bullet, addressing the elephant in the room directly. "It's pretty impossible not to think about our night together, but a woman who might really vomit if I kissed her makes it easier to ignore those memories right now."

Scarlet stole across her face, briefly giving her cheeks some color. "I didn't mean to insinuate that something was going to happen. I know I'm not in danger, I just didn't want to take bigger advantage of your good nature than I already am. And I really hate feeling like an obligation."

Rolling to his side, he stretched out, put his cell on the bedside table, then opened one arm for her. "You're not an obligation. Didn't we go over this earlier?"

"That was hours ago, and maybe even yesterday."

"It was today."

"And I'm such a mess I had to double-check."

She looked at his outstretched arm. "It's kind of breaking my self-esteem that I'm this wretched at only two months pregnant."

He let his arm drop. Whatever she needed from him, it was possible he'd become too tired to riddle it out. "I want to stay."

As he settled, she switched off the light, and despite her declaration what side she slept on, and despite ignoring his offer of a comforting hug seconds before, as soon as he closed his eyes he felt her shifting toward him on the bed and wriggling under the arm he'd offered. Her cheek pillowed on his chest and she wrapped one arm over his waist.

In moments she was asleep and he drifted off right behind her.

CHAPTER FOUR

GABRIEL HAD AWAKENED the middle of the night because she'd made a noise, only to find her bottom was nestled against his groin and the immediate realization of just how far past businesslike the whole situation had gone.

He'd never spooned with another partner. He hadn't told her no relationships because he didn't specifically want *her*, it had been his basic operating system since Nila. He dated, casually. He had lovers, and did not bring them to his apartment because if he went to their beds, he could leave before things got snuggly. Spooning, like sleeping alongside lovers, had ceased to be part of his life along with Nila. It was too intimate, and felt like promises, or declarations that he felt more than he did, or at least was willing to go further than casual.

And this was intimate. And easy. And felt good. Outside winter winds rattled the windows, but the bed was warm, and her hair smelled like honey with just a hint of something smoky.

Probably the fire they'd enjoyed the previous evening. It would be beyond ridiculous to associate her with smoky hotness. Even if she was.

Sighing, he edged back toward his side of the bed and tried to go back to sleep, but he was decidedly less comfortable there, physically and mentally.

After twenty minutes, languishing in a vicious circle of thoughts that most closely resembled an ouroboros, he eased off the bed, took his phone and clothes, and left the door open so he could hear her from downstairs.

Over the next few hours he read everything he could about juvenile dermatomyositis, the one thing he could control right now, to see if he could find answers that would set both their minds at ease.

At first light she came down the stairs, wrapped in a fluffy bathrobe, and curled right up with him on the couch, where she promptly went back to sleep with her head in his lap.

When he'd read every journal and website he

could find about JDM, he slid out from beneath her and headed for the kitchen.

"Did you sleep at all?" She sounded groggy, but when he looked back, she was sitting up.

He slipped his phone into his pocket and stayed at the kitchen island, sitting on a stool there to face her. "I slept fine, but then I woke up and couldn't get back to sleep, so I came downstairs to read."

"Find anything good?" Her sleepy gaze sharpened and she sat up straighter, like it would be better to hear bad news with her best posture employed.

He shook his head in answer.

"You mean you didn't find anything, or what you found wasn't good?"

"I found articles discussing the illness being triggered by viruses and infection, and another stating that it was theorized to have a genetic component, but nothing to suggest the alleles responsible had been identified, only hypothesized about," he explained, and she relaxed back into the sofa cushions again, which seemed like a good reaction. "Which means you might not even be able to pass it on."

"But I still may be able to."

Although still sluggish, she got off the sofa and made her way into the kitchen. "Can you show me the ratios on tea to cider, so you don't have to keep waiting on me for tea? I think I want some toast too. It feels like a day with food in it."

"Take your antiemetic and wait twenty minutes. Just in case?" But what bothered as much as it pleased was the easy domesticity that continued between them. First sleeping. Then spooning. Then breakfast together, sleepy smiles over tea and toast.

He knew what she'd call it, or maybe he didn't know the exact words, but he knew the gist. It was simply them falling into the New Family pattern. He struggled to even wrap his mind around the definition. Family meant something precise to him, and that wasn't this, no matter what he was going along with right now.

Toast and tea went down easily enough, and before the morning was through she was asleep again on the sofa.

Now coming on afternoon, he'd done everything he could think to do to keep from going stir crazy. His research had wandered from diseases to custody, the rights of fathers in New York. That led him to contact a lawyer to arrange a meeting so that he could start the process to draw up papers.

And now he was again out of things to keep busy. The more time he spent in her presence, especially when not busy and unobserved, the more his thoughts strayed into dangerous territory. Like those first awkward days when he couldn't close his eyes without flashes of their night together singeing the pleasure-seeking parts of his brain.

The silken skin he'd become reacquainted with last night.

The remarkable—he now knew—strength in her slender feminine frame. How she'd gripped him with her thighs in the dim candlelit shower. Her heat against him, around him, when the tile wall had been so cold.

He alternated between mindless fantasies and the ones that formed around shared holidays and vacations, with warm-skinned, blue-eyed children running around. It could work, he knew it could. She wanted him physically, she liked him—she hugged him too much to discard the notion that she was actually fond of him.

They needed to talk about this stuff, once she could stay awake long enough for conversation. Until then, he needed something to do. To distract himself, he went to the bookcase lining the far wall of the living area and prowled the shelves.

Organized by color, genres mixed together, she had a little of everything. But there was a shelf in the center that didn't match the others, having spines of every color poking out. Thick spines, leather bound, embossed decoration… Photo albums.

He pulled the first one out and clawed into it, looking for some sort of focus, some sort of decency.

Pictures from last year's work holiday drinks looked like a good place to start.

There would be no pictures from this year's holiday get-together, as Penny hadn't made it to the pub earlier in the week, and he'd pointedly not asked why. Not coming to a pub made more sense now—she'd said she'd suspected for a while. Making understood his unwillingness to speak about their night had been a mistake, and one he wasn't going to make again. They had to talk about this stuff, no matter how worked up either of them got. It was an emotional subject, they were bound to get emotional, but if she wasn't talking to him, he couldn't fix whatever went wrong before it spiraled out of control. He didn't want to miss something like that, like he'd missed with Nila.

Even now, none of that made sense to him. They'd grown up together, became high school sweethearts, dated on and off in college, and then really got back together at the joint barbecue their parents had thrown to celebrate each of them graduating university. Dating exclusively, marriage in medical school, and divorce in residency. Now, having had years to examine it, he still couldn't point to any symptoms of a marriage dying.

Snagging four other albums, he tucked them under his arm and went to sit down to look at something besides the glowing screen giving him a headache since the middle of the night.

The department party photos flowed on to another Christmas scene, and he realized it was moving backward in time. She'd been out of the country last Christmas, so this had to be the year before that.

There organization disappeared after just a few pages. He expected another Christmas, but he got somewhere sunny. Different Davenports graced the pages, and he looked a little closer every time he saw a face he knew. How people spent their holidays said a lot about them. What could these pictures tell him about his child's future family parties?

Were there clues here that he could spot to help him understand Penny better than he already did? Nila's leaving had changed that about him, he paid attention to everything now. Everyone. He examined not just the external but the glimpses he got of the internal. Those glimpses just didn't show enough to make him feel comfortable with any of this.

And the pictures? Well, he could see the Davenports summered in the Hamptons. Fourth of July came with a beach party of some kind. New Year's Eve was always somewhere that glittered. In every picture, the Davenports always appeared perfectly presentable, precisely as he'd have expected.

It was the family Christmas parties he kept stopping at. Something bothered him about those photos. They looked like magazine spreads. Perfectly polished. The trees sparkled but had no personal touches he could see, unless they'd gathered as a family to learn how to blow glass and make ornaments.

It had probably been erected by a hired hand who'd picked every piece for beauty, not for sentimentality. Did the fabulously wealthy decorate their own trees or bake their own Christmas cookies?

He'd liked all the Davenports he'd met, so picking out, or possibly manufacturing flaws for these perfectly good people left a bitter taste in his mouth.

He flipped that album closed and reached for the next in his stack.

This one was both more interesting and more alarming. It looked like Penny's Book of Dangerous Stunts.

Pictures of her racing a horse.

Pictures of her steering a parachute in for a landing.

Pictures of Penny the white-water rafter. The derby-car driver. The hang glider.

Penny caught by the belt by Charles Davenport as she dangled over the safety railing at Niagara Falls, her hands reaching for the water!

That one was older, but no more than a decade, and he could feel his expression mirroring the look he saw on Charles's face—brows down, mouth open and horrified, and *angry.*

He snapped that album closed before his head exploded.

"Hey," she said from the couch, sitting up, her face also mirroring Charles's.

"Are you all right? Did I wake you?"

She ignored his questions, looked at the albums, her head tilted to see the colorful spines, then suddenly catapulted off the sofa to stumble over to snatch up the remaining albums. No words, she just hauled them right back to the shelf where he'd found them.

And didn't even seem to notice that in her haste she'd stepped in one of her buckets and it was still on her foot.

"Glad those are clean," he murmured.

Something she might also be thankful for when she realized her foot was in a pail.

Which hadn't happened yet.

She just turned to look at him. "Don't look at these. Old photo albums are off-limits."

That tranquil bubble that had been making him too comfortable all morning evaporated, which he was thankful for, but not enough to stop himself trying to understand. This was one of those glimpses.

"Why?" He stood up and when she clomped back to him, took her by the hips and lifted her up, booted the bucket out of the way, and set her back on her feet. "You've been wearing your barf bucket like the ugliest shoe in history."

Coming out of a dead sleep and launching herself across the room wasn't great for her powers of perception. But when her feet touched the cool wood floors, the sleepy haze started to lift. "These pills... I don't know what's worse, the nonstop vomiting without them or the nonstop sleep with them."

"You'll get used to them. In a few days you'll be able to stay awake."

She made some disgruntled sound and pulled

away so she could put the remaining albums back, he realized. It was the fastest she'd moved in days, speeding from the chair to the bookshelves.

"What's the point of albums if you don't let people look at them?"

"They're ugly," she argued, then took two specific albums and wedged them behind the others so they were trapped between the books and the wall and not immediately visible, as if he hadn't seen her put them there.

"You don't want anyone seeing your awkward puberty photos?"

She sighed, then sagged against the shelves, but when she looked at him he could see clarity returning to her.

"I don't want *you* to see those pictures. You don't see me like that." She straightened and walked back much more sluggishly, as if all the energy she'd had moments before was gone. "You know I was ill, but when you look at me you don't see that girl. Poor little Penelope. You see Penny, pilot and paramedic, energetic and… maybe sometimes too impulsive. But you don't *pity* me. You don't look at me and think, can she physically do this or that?"

The rawness in her voice gave the words sense they wouldn't have otherwise had.

"You can tell me you were terribly ill, but you don't want me to see it."

"There are very few people in my life I'm close to—you and my sister, Miranda, basically—who don't see the long shadow Penelope casts when looking at me, and I don't want you to see me that way. I want you to see me how I am now, or how I was before all this. Strong. Capable. Healthy. Not perpetually nauseous."

She'd just included him in a small group that consisted of him and her *sister*, the one member of her family who apparently only knew New and Improved Penny.

"Sit down before you fall down." He gestured back to the sofa, then sat back in his chair.

He was in the box of people who saw her as complete. Boxes he could understand. He liked them. If you put people into one box you kind of knew what to expect from them. It kept things neat.

Or it would if he could figure out what box to

put her into. She kept moving. Partner. Lover. Possible wife. Mother of his child. The boxes were overlapping, which defeated the whole point of boxes.

But she'd just put him into a box with family. Was that New Family? It couldn't be that easy.

"I feel terrible. I've been letting you take care of me every second of the day so the least I could do is help with dinner." Despite her words, Penny edged onto a stool at her kitchen island and watched Gabriel continue chopping sweet potatoes he'd just peeled. "What is it we're having again?"

"Simple grilled chicken breast, since your kitchen is awesome, and baked sweet potato wedges. Everything I've read said take it easy on vegetables for a few days."

There had even been some kind of marinade for the chicken, which automatically announced that he was a better cook than she was. The very best Penny ever managed in the kitchen when starting from a position of raw food was fondue. She could melt a mean pot of cheese and buy a mean loaf of bread. She also reheated meals from restaurants like a master.

His proficiency shouldn't gall her, but somehow it did. It seemed like he did everything well, except maybe relax. He hadn't relaxed anytime she'd been awake and watching him. Even when he'd said he was tired, he'd still dug into her albums rather than just lean back and have a nap like any sane, overworked New Yorker would.

"I'm feeling better than I did. I'm going to try and go back to work tomorrow."

"Are you sure you're ready?"

"On the floor. The floor is safe. If I'm working in Emergency and I start vomiting, I can just go home. No crash landings to sort out first."

"Sensible," he praised. "Sensible" in Gabrielese was like "awesome" in Penny's world.

She changed the subject before all that praise went to her head. "Did your mom teach you to cook?"

"Grandmother. Mom's mom. My mom's a great cook too, but I learned to cook from my grandma. Spent a lot of time with her in the summer when my parents were still working and we needed minding."

"We?" She didn't have any cozy grandma stories, but that wasn't the part of the statement that interested her. "You have siblings?"

He tossed the potato wedges with oil to coat them, spread them on a baking sheet, salted and peppered, and then shoved them into a pre-heated oven. The show-off.

"No siblings. Cousin. We were as close as siblings but, uh, not now."

She knew next to nothing about his past, and her plan to learn about it two months ago hadn't exactly worked as planned. "Did he move away?"

Everything was on to cook, and Gabriel took his time washing his hands again as they shimmered with oil, and then he turned back to her. "He died a couple of years ago."

The manner of delivery was flat, like he didn't care at all, but that wasn't possible, not when he'd previously referred to him as close as a sibling. That didn't add up.

"I'm sorry."

"Me too."

"Do you want to talk about it?"

He gestured to her untouched cup of apple tea and, before answering, grabbed tongs to flip the chicken breasts over on the grill built into her neglected but terribly fancy range. "There's not much to tell. We weren't close when he died. In junior high, he got involved with the wrong crowd, and it went downhill from there."

The wrong crowd. Downhill. And Gabriel was from New Jersey... "Was he murdered?"

"It was an accident, actually. But he was shot. Wrong place, wrong time."

"Like a store robbery gone wrong?"

He put the tongs down and looked over his shoulder at her. "What made you ask that specifically?"

Penny shrugged, took a sip of her tea so he didn't tell her to drink it again, and it gave her time to work out why she'd chosen that random situation. "You said he went with the wrong people, and then later got accidentally shot because he was in the wrong place, which implies innocence. It was the first thing that popped into my head where an innocent bystander could be shot. You hear about convenience store robberies all the time. Was I right?"

Nodding, and looking a little disconcerted, he

came to lean against the other side of the island. "Sometimes your instincts alarm me."

"My gut talks to me. Unfortunately, the past couple days most of what it's been saying has been… 'Let's get all this food out of here.'" She pointed to her belly then her mouth, and when he grinned, she shrugged. "This is why I could never have been a doctor. I like to skip over parts of the whole logical progression of facts. I usually get the right answer, but I also rarely have any real idea how I got there. Whenever they told me to show my work in math classes, I was always in trouble. Got the right answer usually, and never had a complete breakdown of the steps. I could get several of the steps, usually in order, but I always missed writing down some."

"That's why you didn't go to medical school like all your siblings?"

"Nope. I didn't want to go to medical school. Can you imagine me studying that much? I can't. Plus… I had been confined for so long that, once I could, all I wanted to do was keep moving. I didn't even want to go to school as long as it would take to become a physical therapist. I'm not dumb, I just can't sit still that long when I'm not drugged by anti-barf pills. Why did you become a doctor?"

"Because the human organism is fascinating. And it's good to help people when and how you can. And body parts are easier to fix than mental parts. I originally thought I'd go into psychiatry, I wanted to figure out where things went wrong for Kyle." He peeled the chicken off the grill, then went to fetch the potatoes, and when he came back, his brows had come down in such a firm line that she didn't know whether to ask him to expand on his statement.

All she knew was that Kyle was his cousin.

"When did you change track?"

"The first time he went to jail, I went to visit with him to try and tackle this problem, work out some way to get him to change his own track, and he said the best part of his childhood was when we stayed with Grandma in the summer. I knew why, even though he didn't try to explain it, and that I couldn't help him fix it."

She didn't prod at the wound until they'd dished up plates and relocated to her ever-neglected dining room to eat like civilized people, with her taking a nibble-the-potato-and-see-what-happens approach to eating.

He doled out information slowly, and she was sensitive to making emotional missteps with him, at least outside wrestling her albums away from him. Those were only a fraught subject for her. She waited until dinner was half-over, deciding what and how to ask before she prodded that wound again, gently. "What was wrong with the rest of Kyle's childhood?"

"He didn't have a dad. His mom worked all the time to support them. She loved him and tried to do what was best for him, but he didn't have what I had. A stable home life, the love and support of both parents." He winced a touch, as if knowing how out of step with modern life he sounded, then clarified, "Little boys need fathers to teach them how to be a man. He didn't have that, so he found that instruction from other places. Not good places."

The subject came with gravity, of course it was heavy, but his pauses were just as heavy. There was something else going on in his mind.

Putting down her remaining half a potato wedge, she carefully wiped her fingers, then reached for his hand. "I know I'm not always su-per-present and good at picking up on social cues, but I'm on the job tonight. There's something you want to say, and you can stop drip-feeding it to me. Just say it. That mutual agreement not to talk about stuff has *got* to go if we're going to have any hope of making this work."

He listened, and she liked the way he paid at-tention, like every word she said—or sometimes babbled—was important. When she tugged on his thumb, he turned his hand over, fingers open-ing so she could slide hers into them.

"Whatever is making you retreat into your head, spit it out."

"I'm trying to be careful about all this. You want to know what's going on in my head? We're making another massive mistake."

Her stomach lurched and wobbled, but since nothing immediately rushed up her esophagus, she stayed put and tried to breathe through it. "What mistake?"

"I still want to marry you. I don't understand how this parental partnership will work out."

"I thought it was pretty self-explanatory. We'll

be parents, and share stuff. The baby. Responsibilities. Decisions."

"Yes, that's self-explanatory. It's the rest of it."

"What rest?"

He jiggled their intertwined hands.

The relationship stuff. Not the actual parenting. The undefined partnership aspect.

"Oh."

"I only know how to do that one way. The traditional way. Raising children with a wife, making a family."

"We'll still be a type of family."

"No, we won't. We'll be two people who share a family member. At best, we'll be like some kind of in-laws, quasi-related because of another."

"We're going to have legal paperwork for custody."

"Which is what you get after a divorce, when you stop being a family. When you're a *broken* family."

The words sank in slowly, along with the understanding that it meant something to him. The words "broken family" and his tone said enough. There was pain there.

"Did your parents divorce when you were little?"

"They're still happily married."

Which, maybe, provided the blueprint, but didn't explain the pain she saw on his face. Was it to do with Kyle?

"But there's someone who divorced."

"Me." There was a flash of something on his face, but she couldn't name it, only recognized it as a cocktail of something unpleasant, maybe painful, definitely sad. "I'm divorced. A long time now. I wanted kids with her, she said she didn't, then didn't want me either. Smothering her or ignoring her, I never got a good answer—it changed, depending on the day. She left."

He delivered the words simply, even somehow without emotion except for his volume. She knew without him saying so how deeply it had cut him by his volume. His ever-decreasing volume. By the time he'd said "She left," it was almost a whisper.

He'd been hurt, and she hated that this hurt him more. The only parts of this conversation that felt good was the fact that they were talking, and his warm hand linked with hers.

Maybe he was right, maybe it was ridiculous to think they could have a simple partnership, there was too much *something* between them. History? Chemistry? Genuine caring? But the answer to that big riddle wasn't in her gut. The only thing in her gut was the desire to give something back to him that he'd been giving her the past two days—comfort, acceptance.

The day it had all gone down, and he'd come over to find her wallowing in guilt after beaning him with the test, his hand on her cheek had been enough to cleave through the swirling *awfulness* in her heart, and ground her.

Extracting her hand from his, she rose and rounded the corner of the table to stand behind his chair. If those pills hadn't sucked all her energy up, she'd have just muscled his chair back from the table and planted herself in his lap so she could hug him until he felt better. But with her current energy level she might have chicken and sweet potatoes on her plate, but there wasn't any strength there.

"Pen?"

"Shhh," she answered softly, then wrapped both her arms around his shoulders and pressed against the seatback, until his head rested against her collarbone and her cheek pressed to his head.

"I know I can't make that better. If I had a time machine, I would go back in time and stop you from marrying that terrible person."

His chest deflated a little, tension not entirely gone but diminishing. She kissed the top of his head then his temple, letting her lips linger there. Would he feel the same melting sweetness she'd felt when he'd kissed her head?

He breathed out so slowly and deeply she could only tilt her head to try and catch his eye, with no idea what any of it meant.

She'd no sooner stepped from behind his chair than it slid back. His large hands found her cheeks and drew her mouth down to his. Just like the first time in that Schenectady motel room, her whole world narrowed down to just her and Gabriel. Her body moved without conscious thought, bringing her to sit across his lap as he angled his head to accommodate the change in height and keep their mouths from separating.

Nothing about Gabriel's kisses could be called hurried, and he never let her hurry him either. Her whole life was rushing for the finish line, grabbing life and experiences before they could get away from her, but no matter how she clutched at his shoulders, or twisted her hands in his shirt to try and pull closer, he held her still. His hands fisting in her hair held her back enough to force her to focus on the slow, velvety slide of his lips on hers. His tongue in her mouth was a dance, slow and drugging. Smoky and potent, it singed the hard edges of their painful conversation and curled the corners like burnt paper.

She didn't know how long it went on, only that at the last gentle, sweet kisses trailing off, she was breathless and in trouble. Passion was still there, but this was something else entirely. Sweet, exploring, consoling, vulnerable, and all she really wanted was to pull tighter and hold onto him, let whatever wanted to happen happen. Stop trying to force words or expectations onto whatever *this* was.

Only that plan hadn't worked so well for their night together, even less after their night in Schenectady, not knowing what to say. Relationships came with expectations, and expectations came with disappointment, pain.

Asking him to stay another night would be a mistake. Asking him to sleep with her in the bed until morning would be a bigger mistake. Gabriel needed the comfort that his expectations could be satisfied, and she couldn't give him that.

"I think I need to sleep," she said instead, not mentioning the kiss or the way pulling away from him left an ache in her chest. Really not inviting him to stay until he didn't want to stay anymore, be it twenty minutes or twenty years. "It'll be an early morning."

"I'll clean this up."

"No, it's okay. I have someone coming tomorrow. Leave it."

She hurried away from him while trying to seem like she wasn't fazed by what had just happened, then climbed the stairs, leaving the decision to him on how to handle the night.

As she shut off the bedside light to settle into bed, she heard his decision in the closing of her apartment door. He'd left, whatever that meant.

CHAPTER FIVE

"WHAT'S WRONG WITH YOU?"

Penny had just thrown back her head to take her don't-barf-today pill when her brother's voice almost made her choke on the darned thing. Carefully, she swallowed, took another big drink from her tumbler of apple tea, and smiled, probably like she'd just been caught doing something bad, because that was exactly opposite to the kind of smile she was going for.

But, really, what had Zac seen? He'd caught her taking a pill alone in the staffroom. So what?

"Vitamin."

Lying to family was a great way to start your day.

"Really? Have you been grounded because of multivitamin dependency?"

Smart-alec brothers were a less great way to start the day. Not having a story primed to tell people she didn't yet want to know she was pregnant? Also a fairly un-great way to start the day.

"I'm not grounded," she denied, tugging at her scrubs, wishing like heck for her comfy flight suit. "I decided to work the floor for a couple days. That's all."

The look he gave her demanded more words, but she couldn't think of any.

"Really." It wasn't even a question. Questions had a questioning lilt. His word just sat there like a big disbelief log for her to trip over.

"Sometimes I work in the department. You know paramedics are good on the floor." And none of this was making her less guilty, especially since she could feel her cheeks getting hot. "Charles said it was okay."

"Why? Something to do with how pale you are?" Then his brows snapped down like a plank over his eyes. "What's going on?"

"Fine, I got hold of something that made me throw up a lot." Not exactly a lie. Everything made her throw up a lot.

"Are you hungover?"

Hungover. God, why did everyone think she

was such a mental case that she'd be drinking heavily when she had to work the next day?

On second thoughts, better that story than the other.

"Not anymore. But you're right, it was tequila. I met this guy, we did some body shots, and then after all the loud, sweaty sex on the jungle gym in his bedroom, then we did some more body… Hey, Zac, where ya goin'? I was just getting to the good part!"

She felt herself grinning at his retreating back, and then chuckling because that look of abject horror? Yeah, that was the stuff littler sisters *lived* for.

But then she remembered Gabriel, and it got a lot less funny. She didn't want to have crazy jungle gym sex with some strange bar guy, but she could easily be talked into that with Gabriel. Though he'd never have a jungle gym. Not that he needed one.

And just like that she felt guilty about the whole thing again. Not just that she'd made up a silly story to Zac, but that she'd lied to him in such a way as to make him as uncomfortable as she was to push him off the subject. She'd never felt bad about messing with him before so she was going to blame this one on the baby. Her judgy, judgy baby.

With a sigh, she stashed her tumbler in a cabinet where it'd stay warm for hours and went to find Zac. It was time for her shift to start anyway.

She buzzed into the department from the east, and after a check of the board headed off in the direction she hoped to find Zac, and nearly ran right into Gabriel with Lawson, wheeling a patient in on their gurney.

"Hey." She scrambled back, but then looked at the patient—a man with a rod of rebar piercing his right shoulder. It took her a moment to get a grip. "Did you call in to get him assigned?"

Gabriel nodded over her shoulder and she turned in time to see Zac and Dr. Ella Lockwood scuttling toward them, along with a team bringing up the rear. She wasn't needed here, so she stepped back out of the way and let them go past.

As they returned to wheeling their obviously pained patient past and Gabriel started reporting the full situation, he locked gazes with her for just a second, but didn't pause either his steps or his words.

He just looked like…

I see you.

I wish you were in the air with me.

Are you okay?

She saw all that, and only had time to smile, and then her own comm was buzzing and it was time for her to go the opposite direction, and babysit a tachycardic patient to Imaging with a cardioversion machine, just in case. Not as dull as being on the floor could be, but subdued enough that she was glad she had this Gabriel business to think about so she wouldn't keep imagining herself yelling "Clear!" and performing chest compressions.

The day dragged on for years, and by the time Penny got home she was only moderately proud of not having vomited at work. Moderately, because she knew she might not have been playing show and tell with the day's menu, but she still wasn't at her best. She was tired. Tired in a way that she'd been hoping would pass. Tired in a way that left her wondering if the wonderful terrible pills were the culprit or if it was just a new fact of life for the next several months.

Her apartment was dark and empty, just as she

knew it would be but had still secretly hoped to be surprised about.

But who actually did that kind of thing? Besides someone who had a key to get in? Even if he had, he couldn't be not only over-the-top romantic but also telepathic enough to know she wanted it when she hadn't told him. If he had been there, without a key, without an invitation, she'd tell anyone else it was time for a restraining order. Instead, she was fantasizing about being stalked.

Because, no matter what she'd been saying about not wanting to be in a relationship, they were already in a relationship. Some kind of relationship. And she liked it. More than that, she looked forward to seeing him in a way that meant every second she spent in a corridor in Emergency was a second she spent looking up and down, hoping to see his broad shoulders and long stride, eating up the floor.

She missed him.

Fishing out her phone, she wavered between calling him and texting.

Texting felt safer.

Again with the courage deficiency. Run toward the scary thing. Run toward it.

She dialed Gabriel's number, and just before hitting the little green button to actually call she lost her nerve.

She texted instead.

You busy tomorrow night? Thought we might do something.

Gabriel rang the bell to Penny's door twenty minutes ahead of when he was due to arrive. It had only been two days since he'd been there, but it felt much longer. At the same time it didn't feel like long enough.

That kiss had crossed a line. At no time since all this had started had he felt like he was in control of anything. And he didn't know what to do with any of it. He also didn't know whether this was a date or just a meeting to discuss responsibilities.

He hoped responsibilities. She already made him feel too good, her apartment felt too good. Too relaxed. Too inattentive.

As unlikely as it was, if she just married him he'd feel so much better. He wouldn't have to doubt her sincerity about the baby. He'd have the law on his side too. Yes, he was rushing things, but as much as he trusted her with his life every day in the chopper, he couldn't find it in himself to trust her with *his child*. Even if his gut told him that fear was somewhat silly.

She wouldn't do anything on purpose to cause it harm, and she'd said she wanted him involved, but…

Nila.

Nila. Nila. Nila.

Where was she?

He pressed the bell again, and seconds later heard thundering feet inside the cavernous loft.

Well enough to run. Good.

"Hey," she greeted him before she even had the door fully open, and her bright smile said she was happy to see him.

"Sorry I'm a bit early." He saw she had on full make-up, which was unusual for her, and didn't seem to be dressed yet. "But I dressed warmly, as you said."

"I see. I need to get dressed still and do something with my hair. Probably braid it so it will go under a knit cap. Otherwise I'll freeze. But

I got you something." She gestured him inside, and darted to the kitchen counter to pick up a tiny gift box, which she held out with a smile so wide he could've counted all her teeth.

Outdoors. Probably ice skating or a walk in Central Park... Both of which were *dates.* This was a date.

A date with a gift. After closing the door, he turned back to eye the box and her bright, shining smile, and carefully took the slim, white, bowless box. "Why did you get me a gift? What is it?"

"It's a car," she deadpanned, then just shook her head. "Open it. It's not like I went out and paid a gazillion dollars for something. It's a... Oh, goodness. Do you have an aversion to surprises? I didn't throw it at your face this time."

When he moved his hand, something hard inside the box slid into the side wall with a thunk, and he shrugged through the weirdness to open the lid.

Inside sat a key with a pewter stethoscope keyring. On the inside bottom of the box was a series of numbers written in purple ink.

"It's for the door. I know how close you were to breaking it down that first day I missed work.

The code is for the security system. You can change it if you want to, but I just..." She stopped as he pulled the key from the box, brows up, and he could see a shadow of anxiety there in her beautiful blue eyes.

What could he say? The little keyring was thoughtful, but the key? The key was two inches of shining, silvery hope. "I was seconds from putting my shoulder into it, though now that I've seen the thing from the inside, I'm fairly certain all I could've accomplished was hurt my shoulder."

"I probably should've waited until later to give it to you, but we don't always end things on an even keel, do we? I wanted to make sure you knew that my heart was in the right place. I know we both have all this...baggage, and your wife wasn't on the level with you, but I need you to know that I am," she said, her voice softer than before, tentative even when she typically charged forward with such energy, "It's not an engagement ring, but it *is* an invitation."

Now he really didn't know what to say. He looked at the numbers she'd written down. Six digits in sets of two, separated by hyphens. It was a date. Two months ago. His chest tightened as the implication hit him. That was the date they'd spent in the motel. Not just numbers to dial in but an acknowledgement that these particular numbers were important. It was a promise.

"Thank you." His voice sounded creaky to him, and the words wholly inadequate.

He'd taken so long to talk, she'd already reached the stairs to go and finish getting ready, but she stopped with her foot on the first step to look back at him, and held his gaze.

"What do you mean by invitation?"

"To move in."

Three words, and then she left him there with it, jogging up the stairs to get dressed.

Move in.

His heart began to pound, and he walked to the sofa to sit. It wasn't marriage, it wasn't security, it wasn't legally binding, but it was a step. Tonight was a date, but it was also to be a discussion about the future. Not just having fun outdoors. She was trying to meet him halfway.

By the time her feet sounded once again on the stairs, he felt more like himself. He'd threaded the keyring onto his own keys and familiarized himself with the security panel again.

She had braided her hair in pigtails that came from beneath either side of a thick, wooly hat, and had on jeans, boots, a coat, scarf, a bag slung across her torso, and had gloves in her hand. "Are you ready? We have to get a cab to Rockefeller Center, there's a children's choir singing tonight near the tree. Then I thought we could grab something to eat, if all is going well in belly-land."

He should say some words before they left but just didn't know where to begin. To keep her from getting away, he caught her hand before she wiggled it into her glove and stepped closer. The times he'd touched her face, she'd stopped dead in her tracks, so that would have worked, but it also seemed to short-circuit her brain in a way that felt like conniving to abuse, especially right now when it felt like they were suspended over Fifth Avenue on a tightrope.

"Do you want me to move in? Is that what your invitation is, or is that your way of saying I'm welcome, whatever is going on with us?"

His little chatterbox didn't answer for long enough he knew words were as big a struggle for her on this, but she did open her fingers to lace them with his and tilted her head back so she could look him in the eye. When she did speak, her voice was soft. "I think we have to name this *whatever is going on with us* a relationship at this point. I didn't want it, you didn't want it, I get that. But it just is… Isn't it?"

"It does seem that way," Gabriel said, then nodded toward the door. "Children's choir, eh?"

Penny couldn't tell whether that abrupt transition meant anything. There should be a relationship manual for idiots to read.

"Linda's grandson." She went with it, naming one of the women in Dispatch, and tilted her head up to him, still uneasy, hungry for some sign on his face of his thoughts. All she knew for sure was that his hand felt good in hers, she'd missed having him around, and this was the most nervous she'd felt in years. Even more uneasy than she'd been when she'd made the decision and boxed up the key earlier. Now that the words were out there, this all became something that could snap back on her and make her regret. "But we can just stop by there and then go have something to eat. I haven't been to see the tree yet this year, and it's there…"

He shook his head then placed one slow, warm kiss on her lips, just enough to make them tingle, just enough to make her smile, and then pulled the key out of his pocket. "I'll get the door."

"Wait," she said, a playful spark igniting in all the intense tingles. "If we're in a relationship, can I do that anytime I want to?"

The look he gave her was cautiously amused, but he nodded.

Permission given, she reached for his scruffy cheeks and drew him back down for another kiss. This time deeper, mouths open, hungrier. And entirely too short. He lifted his head, smile still in his eyes, emboldening her.

"What about sex? Do I get sex anytime I want it now?"

Then he laughed, "You really are new at this. People usually start out relationships a little slower."

"So that's a no?"

"We're going to be late."

"Fine!" She groaned in melodramatic fashion

and armed the security panel, then stepped out of the loft so he could lock it up.

Him with his keys. Did all this mean he was going to move in? Was he thinking about it? The words were already in her mouth, ready to break free, but Gabriel did things at his own pace, and if sex was off the table, that might be too far too. If this was going to work out—if she was going to show him that they could be together, and be a family, and let things flow naturally without labels and flower arrangements in churches—she had to let him get there at his own pace. Even if hers said, *Hurry. Settle it now.*

Like it was even possible to hurry up and make things flow naturally.

Despite sweet kisses, or the hungry kisses they'd shared, neither of them knew what to do when alone together in the back of a cab. Should she offer him her hand? Should she sit near him? People in relationships did that stuff. She did the best she could and scooted closer so that only the width of a skinny thigh separated them, and silently berated herself for this indecision. The other day she'd had no trouble hugging him. She'd had no trouble even cuddling up to him to go to sleep, but that had been before she'd discovered they'd somehow ended up in a relationship. Now everything felt weird. Good, but weird. And something was bugging her, she just couldn't quite put her finger on what it was. Or what they were. It could be many things, for all she knew.

They made small talk about nothing, cases he'd been on that week without details, and soon enough the car stopped at the corner of Forty-Eighth and Rockefeller Plaza, and they climbed out.

On the way around the block to the tree and ice rink, they stopped at a deli for steaming cups of cider and sandwiches, and finally made it to the plaza just after the children started singing. From their position at the back of a crowd she could see the tree—naturally—but not over the crowd separating them. "Let's sit."

She gestured to a bench close enough to hear the music and far enough they could still speak, and Gabriel went along with it well enough.

"Is it weird for us to eat dinner while kids are singing?" Gabriel asked.

"Not unless they're singing 'Do You Hear What

I Hear?' and the answer is *crunching*," Penny answered, mostly because she was actually hungry for the first time in a few days, and her ham and cheese was calling her name.

He grinned, and though it didn't look like he knew how to do this any more than she did, he turned slightly on the round planter benches so he could see her better, and from the return to his sober, thoughtful expression she could see he was chewing on more than his sandwich.

The kids began singing "O Come, All Ye Faithful" and Penny tried to find her way back to banter, that was something they'd always done well before all these *feelings* had got involved. "Have you ever noticed how many Christmas songs start with 'O' something?"

"'O Little Town of Bethlehem'?" Gabriel played along.

"'O Holy Night.'"

"'O…' What else?"

"'O Come Emmanuel…'" That was the last one she could think of.

"Is that it? Four songs is all we could come up with? The way you put it, I thought we'd have some kind of measurable percentage here. There are probably thousands of Christmas songs out there. I bought wholesale into the notion of you being a Christmas carol librarian," he teased, and she could see happiness crinkling the corners of his eyes. Unshielded, uncontrolled, and the sweetness of the sight of him almost choked her up.

"You've got me confused with the internet. But if you get your phone out to check right now, somewhere an angel will... I don't know, fail to get his wings?" With effort, she kept the playful teasing going, wanting things to stay light and happy. Relationships should probably start that way but theirs hadn't, and she truly wanted him to be happy, whatever happened. "Oh, there should be an 'O Gabriel' song. He's an angel, right? I bet he had some job during Christmas night."

"Gabriel was the one who announced the birth," said the man named for an angel, but who was as sexy as the devil...

And who gave her an idea on how to talk to the rest of the world about their new relationship. "Me and God have this in common, I think."

He looked over his sandwich, brows up, definitely not following her clearly insane segue.

"Someone's going to have to announce that this baby thing is happening. Because, oh— *Oh!* That reminds me. Did anything happen the other day when you gave your rebar patient to Zac and Ella Lockwood? They were having a tense discussion later when I stumbled over them, and I think I saw Ella give Zac the stink-eye. Then I felt even more guilty because when he caught me earlier taking my antiemetic I lied about why I needed it." Penny blurted out a bunch of words, and then stopped and made a little circle in the air with her finger. "That started out one place and then kind of came back to that place, which was the place where I don't know what to tell people about being pregnant, but a little more got wedged in there in the middle."

Gabriel could usually keep up with her sudden changes in conversation, though, so he only grinned as the choir drifted into a sober rendition of "What Child is This?" Naturally. "I noticed you went off the rails. One, I'm not announcing this to your family. Two, yes, I did notice something there. Neither of them wanted to give up the patient, so when I left, there seemed to be a show-down brewing. Three, what did you tell him?"

"I told him that I was hungover on tequila after a night of sweaty jungle-gym sex with a guy I picked up at a bar," she answered directly, in one matter-of-fact breath, even though she felt her forehead growing more and more tense and wrinkled as she spoke. "And that's when I knew we were in a relationship, because after I succeeded in driving my brother away so he wouldn't ask more questions, I felt guilty the rest of the day for fake-cheating on you with a pretend person I had just made up."

The seriousness with which he looked at her made her stomach curdle, but just when she thought she was going to have to cry and run away from the plaza in dramatic fashion, he started to laugh. Not a quiet chuckle like she usually got from him either. He opened his mouth and laughed so loudly from their little perch across the plaza, it almost drowned out the singing.

"Shh." She put her sandwich down and her hand over his mouth as he quieted into less raucous laughter, but his eyes twinkled merrily at her as the loudness ebbed and she pulled her hand away. "Come on, now, it's not *that* funny. What are you even laughing at? What I did to Zac, or that I've been feeling guilty? We have to come up with a plan or everyone's going to be squinting at us at work, just like I spent the day squinting at Zac and Ella!"

"If they can handle you trying to throw yourself over Niagara Falls, I think they can handle this."

"I wasn't trying to throw myself over the falls." For some reason, that seemed like the most important part of his statement to address. Or at least the easiest part. "I'd have needed a barrel for that. I just wanted to put my hands in the water. I wasn't going to let go of the railing, I just was doing it from the other side because I didn't think it through very well. Then Charles panicked and dragged me back—almost dumping me into the river in the process, I might add. I had a better grip on the railing than he thought, but no one really trusted in me to not fall on my face every other day at that point."

"My point is the same, this is hardly something that will knock them for a loop." Then he ticked off on his fingers what he'd no doubt learned from her albums before she'd rescued them from him. "Skydiving. Monster trucks. Crash-up derby..."

"My parents are married but they hate each other, because they can't imagine getting a divorce. Does that tell you anything about how traditional they are?"

"Do they really *hate* each other?"

"Yeah, I'm pretty sure."

"Why?"

"You know, Miranda's existence? Dad's affair and whatever? Mom never got over that one." And Miranda was probably who Penny was closest to, but who she absolutely didn't want to tell that she was having a baby outside marriage. Not that Miranda was judgemental, but with the way things had been, growing up—single mom, no father in the picture until her mom had died—it felt like anything even passably resembling the situation had the chance of hurting her only sister. "I guess things were different earlier, back when they trusted one another, but as soon as that trust went, everything went with it."

He finished his sandwich; hers was half-gone, but she'd lost all interest in it. These discussions could probably even sour a stomach completely devoid of pregnancy hormones.

"Trust is important," he agreed.

She couldn't bring herself to ask whether he trusted her. Clearly, he didn't, if he needed a marriage and documentation as much as he'd claimed. "So, I'm just going to say this, because I don't know how to do this relationship thing. All I can think is that being direct is the best way to go."

"Say what you want to say."

"Okay. I can't say I'll ever marry you, but if I can get to this place where I'm even willing to dip a toe into relationship-infested waters, it's possible I could *eventually* come around to the idea of marriage too. If we do this the right way. Like let it unfold naturally. Figure out how to be together as a couple, not just as two people who made a baby. It's not a promise, I literally hate spending time anywhere my parents are in the same room together. Charles's wedding is coming up, which I need a date for, by the way, but also if you come, you'll see them together. You'll understand what I think of when I think marriage.

I have some other issues because I'm, you know, a basket case."

He let her go on and on, nodding here and there to show he was still keeping up. Of all the people in her life, Gabriel was the only one who would let her babble on for ages uninterrupted, which was another mark in his pro column.

"That's a bunch of I-don't-knows, but here's what I do know. I can't seem to think of you as just my partner anymore. And, to be honest, I haven't been able to since Schenectady."

His expression closed down, and he'd stopped nodding, but she knew he'd heard her. He'd heard every word, she felt it in the gravity of his gaze and the way he reached over to tuck a flyaway strand of hair into her knit hat. "It sounds like they're winding down."

The singing. She went with the redirect and cocked her head toward the music to listen.

"'Carol of the Bells,'" she murmured, gathering up her dinner refuse to dispose of. "Want to go closer to listen? I can't believe they got a bunch of eleven-and twelve-year-olds to learn this complicated a song."

Trash disposed of, confessions made, she held

her hand out to him, needing to test that boundary and know if he'd take her hand in public. When he did, she tucked in close enough to almost lean as they walked back toward the audience to hear the last of the singing.

That first bridge crossed, Gabriel stepped behind her to wrap his arms around her waist, and when she leaned back, she felt pounds lighter. This relationship business was like a dark room and she only had a flickering flashlight. Sometimes she could see a path forward, but then the light went out and left her blindly feeling her way and wondering if she'd just stepped on gum or something worse.

Right now, her flashlight was working. Gabriel stood behind her, his arms around her waist, listening to kids singing Christmas songs while she gazed up at the legendary, glittering tree. In that breath, she could picture it. She could picture glittering Christmas trees in the future, and a chubby-legged toddler with warm brown skin, curly black pigtails and blazing blue eyes. In Gabriel's lap. Not because she wasn't healthy enough to stand on her own but because there was nowhere she'd rather be than on her daddy's knee.

Stinging in her eyes let her know she was going too far into that fantasy, but it was a good step. It was something happy, something *besides* the cold nature Christmases had taken in the Davenport household these past fourteen or so years.

"I ordered a bunch of Christmas decorations for the loft," she said, as much to try and take her mind off that wandering path as to make a sideways approach to including him in it. She'd pretty much used up her daily courage quota, so she couldn't come directly at the question she really wanted to ask. The best she could do was hint and hope he'd just come out and tell her he was going to move in. "Do you think you'd like to come help me decorate this weekend?"

CHAPTER SIX

BY THE TIME Penny got home the next evening, the white sneakers she wore when on the floor scuffed and squeaked across the polished lobby floor, she so failed at lifting her feet fully while walking. Then again off the elevator to her door. Most days in the ER weren't especially exciting for her, but today had been so busy she'd spent the day longing for five minutes just to sit down.

Sliding her key into the lock even felt like a feat of strength. Before she turned the thing, she heard sound through her door. Had she left the television on this morning? Had she even watched television this morning?

That creeping sensation of being watched came up on the back of her neck and stilled her hand. Living alone in New York, she'd developed enough situational awareness to come alert instantly when things seemed out of place. She'd also learned sometimes it was worth looking like a paranoid idiot and getting Security to go into her place with her if she was spooked. Like she suddenly was.

As quietly as she could, she slid the key from the lock and then turned to run for the stairwell, not wanting to wait for the elevator. She could be both brave and *smart* about things like this, which involved running the other way just this once.

Five minutes later, she had the on-site security guard at her door with her keys, opening it. He had a Taser in hand, and when the door swung open, he dashed in like they were on an episode of *COPS*, yelling that he was armed and if anyone was loitering in the apartment, they should make themselves known.

Basically, her worst nightmare.

But then the nightmare got worse. Her apartment glittered with twinkling white Christmas lights strung up the columns near the door, which she hadn't put up. And then she saw him: Gabriel, rising from the floor in front of a massive, half-decorated Christmas tree, hands in the air, one glittering silver ornament dangling from his thumb over his head. "I'm supposed to be here."

Her stomach sank a good five thousand feet.

Gabriel had come and decorated all by himself. He hadn't said anything other than "Maybe" when she'd invited him to decorate with her, but here he was. She'd caused a Taser to be pointed at him for all his effort.

He caught sight of her peeking around the guard and with hands still in the air, ornament dangling, he shrugged. "Surprise?"

Dammit!

This would be the second time she'd had to apologize to him. But first she should stop the guard from Tasering him—then she'd really have to apologize.

"Don't shoot! I'm sorry. This is my fault." She darted around her escort and moved into the line of fire, her back to Gabriel so she could address the guard. "I didn't expect it, but this is Dr. Gabriel Jackson. He has keys now. I just forgot. And I wasn't expecting him, and then I got all stupid, and then…"

"Everything's okay, Miss Davenport?" the guard double-checked, before putting his Taser away.

"Everything's very okay. Thank you for com-

ing with me. I'm sorry for...the fuss." She puffed
and, after sharing an apologetic look with Gabriel and making a mental note to get the guard
something nice for Christmas, she walked him
to the door with more apologies.

Gabriel waited patiently until she'd closed the
door before he asked, "You thought I was an intruder?"

"A little bit," she admitted, chewing her lip.
"I'm sorry. But remember yesterday when I said
I'm lousy at knowing how to have a relationship?
That's *this*. I definitely want you here, I just... I
didn't expect you to come over. Not so quickly.
Last night it just seemed like one big question
mark, and...then you decorated. Oh, my goodness, Gabriel, you didn't have to do all this by
yourself, but it's so beautiful!"

He let it all roll off his back, just nodding and
looking wonderfully rumpled but not at all put
out by the confusion. Even if he'd had a Taser
pointed at him by someone of passing compe-
tence. Then he went with the subject he'd probably planned for all day, knowing him, "Don't
look on the other side of the loft—that's where
the mountain of boxes is living."

She never saw him dressed in casual clothes, not really. Even when he'd been there with her for days, he'd put on slacks every morning. But now he wore jeans. And he wore them fantastically. The white T-shirt he had on was also rumpled, and she could see that he'd had a long day just by the state of his attire. It made him more real. It made him even more attractive, if that was even possible.

Sexy. Right down to the silver glitter that had fallen off the ribbons and ornaments and which would definitely linger in the loft for months, and may need a good scrubbing to get off that rich skin.

Immediately she had mental images of them washing one another, luxuriating in soap-slickened muscles under her hands, and the way his whole body had gone tense when she'd gripped him...

Focus. She looked at the tree, at the fade in and out of the white lights, and tried her best to push memories of their shower out of her head. Even if he needed a shower to get the glitter off him, she couldn't offer to help. She could barely believe he was even there.

"You like it?" He sounded just a little tentative, like she was going to hate it. Like it was even possible that he'd done all this, wasted his whole afternoon. Like he wanted to please her.

"Are you kidding? It's the worst. I mean, I hate it. All the wonderful, glittering lights and big red bows," she said, trying to ignore the warm feelings spreading through her chest, scrambling to find her center, that banter she counted on to help her keep it together. "I love it. Can't believe you did all this. How did you get it done in one day?"

"The tree's not done. But I got here right after you left this morning. Borrowed a ladder from Maintenance." He paused. "You sure you like it? Some things I wasn't even sure what they were, or what to do with them. I improvised. And the tree still needs the rest of the ornaments."

"I love it," she said again, pulling her coat off and dropping it as she jogged straight for him and flung her arms around his shoulders. The man smelled like heaven, if heaven were filled with earthy pleasures. "Thank you. Today was such a dreadful day, I wasn't even sure I had the energy to walk up the stairs to bed. Of course, I was going to detour to the fridge to grab something

and stuff in my face as I crawled up the stairs…
but all the excitement of you being a possible
intruder, and then discovering it's actually *you*,
only adorably dusted in silver sparklies? Even
better. I love it."

His hands fell onto her hips and then he gave
in and hugged her back. Resting her cheek on
his shoulder, she breathed out slowly, instantly
relaxing. Then he began to rock, and being too
relaxed became a danger to the evening that suddenly had become full of possibilities.

"If you keep this up, I'm going to lose my burst
of energy," she murmured. "And possibly sleep
standing up."

"Before dinner?"

His voice was like warm honey to her ears,
and she grinned against his shoulder, no longer
hesitant to ask. "Does this mean you're staying?
Tonight? Moving in?"

"I'm staying. We'll call it a trial run. Still think
we should take things slow," he confirmed,
sounding a little more resolute now, and breaking the spell a little as he let go of her and gestured to something she'd missed entirely in all
the awesomeness that had gone on since she'd

walked into a magical twinkling wonderland-style living room, complete with sugar-frosted boyfriend. "I just dumped my bags in the guest room and came straight downstairs, haven't un-packed at all. Tomorrow, I guess."

Boyfriend.

The word stuck in the front of her brain, and made her smile. He was her boyfriend. That particular word didn't even scare her right now, not like *relationship* did. It came with images of hand-holding and slow dancing under starry skies. That special time before things inevitably blew up.

"Something smells good, other than the cinnamon. Smells meaty. You cooked?"

"I warmed up a pre-cooked turkey breast, and got stuff for good sandwiches. So, I barely cooked, but I thought you did all right with a sandwich last night." He nodded to the blanket. "It'd be nice to have food that doesn't need utensils by the fire."

Romantic.

"This is a date, isn't it?"

He shook his head, and then gave the kind of half-shrug she knew to be man-speak meaning:

Yes, but I don't want to make a big deal of it or even have it spoken about.

"Well, let me go get out of my work clothes." She gave him her best, over-the-shoulder sultry voice. "Just so you're aware, I'm going to put on a negligee."

"I thought we agreed to take things slow." Instantly alarmed.

"By negligee you should understand I mean flannel pajamas in cotton-candy pink." She grinned at him as she headed up the stairs, and saw him shake his head, but he was smiling again.

When she returned, she diverted to the stereo to turn on some light mood music. Christmas music, actually. Christmas music was absolutely necessary for a living room Christmas picnic and conversation. And lower lights. And her fireplace all sparked and roaring. She couldn't fully appreciate the twinkling if the overhead lights were canceling out the glow.

By the time they'd settled with their plates on their knees and her with her now usual mug of hot apple cider tea, she began picking his brain about Jackson family Christmas traditions.

This conversation naturally turned back to Davenport traditions, namely her tradition these past few years: Penny's Christmas Adventure.

"I don't know when it started. I guess around twenty-one? I just never really cared about Christmas. It always felt like someone else's holiday, that it was made for the healthy kids—the kids who had a future."

He frowned over his sandwich, so sharply she knew he was taking her literally.

"No one ever said that to me. That's just how I felt. Years of illness takes its toll. I always had very nice gifts, designed to stimulate my mind, and all I wanted was the toys that would stimulate my body. My siblings got bikes and rollerblades, I got a microscope. And then I got a telescope. New computers. Dolls. Good Lord, the dolls. I hated the dolls."

"Didn't they ask what you wanted?"

"Sure. I just didn't have words to tell them, or the heart to say, 'I want to go play in the snow. I want to go sledding. I want to ice skate and trampoline.' Eventually I got better, but Christmas never dazzled me after that. It was tainted with years of heartbreak. I guess that's why I started traveling. Go somewhere new or somewhere I already loved and hadn't fully explored, have some new adventures... I liked it better than sitting with family by the fire, waiting for some present that would disappoint me. Live life, don't just watch from the sidelines."

He looked at the fire, then back at her. "I thought the fire was nice."

"*This* fire is nice. The company is nicer." She tried not to look too wistfully at him. "Really, it's all nice. I wasn't even sure I was going to be able to make myself decorate. Buying things online is a lot easier than putting them up. It even feels different. Maybe it always feels different when it's your own place."

"What's it feel like?"

"Kind of comforting. Kind of exciting? Kind of like a trial run, like you said. Kind of like a last Christmas for just me before I devote the rest of my Christmases to my child. That's not a complaint, just a framework. I should enjoy it so I know what to give her. Or him. And try not to think of it as limiting my adventures, even if sometimes it feels like my adventuring days might be over."

"They're not."

"That's easy to say. They're at least on hold for a long, long time. I've been trying to think of pregnancy-safe adventures to do around the city, and I don't have many ideas at all. Can't go ice skating. Can't go skiing. I've been training for the Empire State Run-Up, where they do this indoor stair-climbing marathon up the Empire State Building. But… I don't know if I can do that while pregnant. Would climbing eighty-six flights of stairs be dangerous? I don't know."

"I don't know why you want to run up eighty-six flights of stairs."

"I don't know why you *don't* want to. Don't you want to find out if you can do it?"

"We climb stairs for work all the time."

"Not that many floors. And not racing other people. Challenging yourself. Seeing if you're as good as they are, or how far you lag behind."

She didn't even realize how she'd said that, putting herself into a position that was inherently *lesser,* until he frowned.

"I doubt you'll lag behind, but you can talk to your doctor about it when you go. You should. If you want to do it, no matter how silly it is."

She nodded, then waved a hand to him. "Do you have any other pregnancy-safe adventure ideas?"

"I guess not shopping."

"Boring."

"Volunteering for a charity? Going to a soup kitchen?"

"That's nice and I should do more of that, but that's not adventurous."

"Dance class?"

She paused. "Dance class? Like, what kind of dance?"

"Interpretive dance."

That made her laugh, and then made her gesture like an idiot for the fruit salad on the other side of him.

He scooted the bowl to her. "Or couples dancing. The classics."

"Ballroom?"

"Or something more fun. Salsa? Swing?"

"That…might not suck. That could be fun," she said, after rolling it around in her head then popping a grape into her mouth. "Go to Georgia and hike the first part of the Appalachian Trail?"

"Camping and hiking? How far is it?"

"I don't know, like a hundred miles or something."

"That's the first segment of the trail?"

"I don't know. I just know that you can do it, and if you do the whole thing, you end up in Maine."

"Scratch that one. You'd give birth in the woods surrounded by elves, and then they'd take our baby away. Elves are like that."

She laughed again at the man, the serious, sober man who was teasing her. "We wouldn't want that."

"Everything I'm coming up with seems results-oriented. But I'm guessing, based on your album, that you're experience-oriented."

She shifted over to him on the blanket and leaned her back against him. "What results?"

"Photography classes, learning to do different things, practical, tangible things." He slid an arm around her, encouraging her to turn in toward him.

"Knitting?"

"For instance."

"Unless it's some kind of knitting marathon where you compete with people while also running around and playing, I don't want to do it. What about that obstacle course television series about being super-fit?"

"You could for a while. I think you've got about three months before your belly will become un-hideable."

"What else?"

"I don't know. Hot air balloons?"

"Oh, piloting?"

"I was thinking riding…"

She tilted her head back to look up at him. "Still, I like that one. I'm keeping it. I'll research online."

In the firelight, she could see at least fifteen specks of silver glitter sparkling on his cheek and forehead, and it tickled her.

He either felt her grinning up at him or she made a sound because he looked down at her, brows raised with unspoken questions.

"You're just sparkly. I'm not sure you haven't already been to the forest with the elves."

"What does that mean?"

"It means you've got more glitter on you than a tarted-up Tinkerbell." She reached up to try and brush it off his cheek, but the glitter didn't budge.

He rubbed his face too. Still it stuck.

"Did you, by chance, take off your shirt while you were dealing with the glittery things?"

"Why?"

"Because if your chest is all glittery, I have to see it. It's really non-negotiable, I'm afraid. I have a rule—if my boyfriend's chest has glitter on it, I get to see it."

She just slipped the B-word right in there.

The disbelieving laugh he gave her emboldened her. Lifting the front of his shirt, she whisked it up so she could peek at the warm brown skin beneath.

"Penny."

"I can't tell. The light's not getting through the cotton. Take your shirt off."

"No…"

She pulled her head back up and lowered his shirt, trying to decide if he was serious or not.

"What if I do a wolf whistle? Men do that all the time on the street, I know it's code for 'Take Off Your Shirt.' Granted, it's dumb code. I could do catcalls!" Which was when it occurred to her. "Wonder why those two different behaviors are attributed to different animals. And wolves don't whistle. Unless they have a sinus condition maybe."

He laughed again then, and didn't even attempt to stop her when she lifted his shirt. His arms went up, he pulled it over his head, and glitter that had been clinging to the cotton fluttered down like little snowy diamonds.

That landed on his chest.

And abs.

And those freaking *hip flexors*...

She slid her hand over his skin, unable to not touch him, just a little mesmerized by the combination of his sparkling flesh and sensation sparking over her own.

It might have started out as playful flirting, but she swung a fuzzy, flannel leg over his lap, getting close, wanting closer. Desperate for his mouth, she'd gotten right up to his, could feel the scruff from his upper lip against hers before she found her willpower. With already accelerated breath, a body aching with anticipation, she leaned back enough to look at him.

Even if he'd played along with the shirt, even if he was going to stay for a trial run, he'd said no sex earlier. And there were things she didn't know, things she needed to understand, and one of them was his boundaries.

As she leaned back, he leaned forward, his gentle hands cupping her cheeks, his wonderful lips brushing hers, beckoning her to forget the words she needed to say. It was the lightest brush, teasing, tempting, and powerful enough to set her heart to hammering.

Nothing could bring her to pull back from him, so it was against his lips, between kisses, that she asked, "What changed your mind?"

The question took his attention and he looked her in the eye. "Changed my mind about what?"

"Between last night and this morning, what made you decide to come for the trial run with me?"

His brows pinched, what she might have called regret in his eyes as he held her gaze. "I knew last night. The instant that key was in my hand. But I wanted to take my time, to think it over."

Did he regret waiting, or was it too soon to regret this? "Were you just trying to be sensible?"

That took him a little longer to put into words, and she saw him look long and hard at her mouth, like he was considering just kissing her again rather than answering.

"It's that bad?"

The quiet ticked on, and whatever words he was running through his mind didn't seem to be lining up the way he wanted. "Because you're—"

A sharp, frosty stab to her chest came with his words.

Criticism was coming. No wonder he couldn't think of the words. She moved back a little further, still on his lap but leaning in the other direction so their torsos made a V. "I'm what? Untrustworthy?"

"I didn't say that."

"You say it all the time. Just not out loud." And she knew it, she heard it every time the thought crossed his mind. Why it hurt so much this time, she couldn't say, but it was there, rotting in her chest. She twisted to the side to climb off his lap.

"You don't trust me explicitly either." His hands gripped her hips and he pulled her back, not letting her get away that easily. A dissatisfied breath rushed out of him and he grunted, "What I was going to say was you make me want to trust… this. You. Last night, you said a lot of things about what you could and couldn't give, and I'm trying to be that resolute, to find some kind of compromise here when it goes against every instinct I have. Because I don't just want this child, I want you. And I don't."

When he'd pulled her back, his firm hands on her hips had brought her into closer contact with his body in ways she was trying not to make contact with while they negotiated boundaries. He wanted her, and he didn't, which pretty much summed up her feelings on the matter too, only she was trying to confront her own issues on this, to make this work.

"Are we just incompatible? I told you I need time and for this to develop naturally, but my trust issues aren't quite the same as yours. I don't trust *marriage* as a concept more than I don't trust *you.* Sure, I think you're probably going to get to a point where you don't want me to be who I am, but I think that about *everyone.* You seem to think I'm going to lie to you, or trick you until I can one day…run off and take the baby and go somewhere you can never find us."

"I'm not saying I just expect that. I'm saying… it's possible. I don't know."

She grabbed his head to make him look her in the eye. "Tell me what you need. Promises? Do you want to put off the trial period until we've been to lawyers to have custody agreements drawn up? Do you want me to write out a declaration of my intent, of your paternity, in longhand right now and sign it? Would that make this feel…less like you're dangling over Niagara?"

"I don't know." He sighed, reaching for her hands to draw them down from his head, a gentle touch as he continued to hold them in the cradle of their joined laps. "I really don't know. But I'm trying."

He was there, she reminded herself, but he'd dragged it out over a night because he genuinely expected this to backfire.

"I need a promise from you," she said, because all she could do was be blunt and direct in this. Every voice in her head that shouted to retreat was a test of her courage, and she couldn't think of anything more important to be courageous about. "I need you to promise that you won't try to make me into someone else. And the other thing, the promise I make to you—if this isn't working, if I decide you're not the one for me,

I promise I'll tell you quickly, end it humanely, not let it drag us to hell to keep up appearances."

"Pen..."

She did climb off his lap then and didn't stop until she was a good foot away, far enough that she felt only the heat of the fireplace at her back, not the warmth of his big body beneath her. "And I promise never to take your child from you unless you do something abusive. If you can put nasty caveats on my future actions—like thinking I'd steal your child from you—I can put caveats on the possibility that you might one day turn into an abusive ass rather than just one unwilling to trust me when I've done nothing to earn that."

His hands flew up and rubbed over his head to the back of his neck. "You went from kissing to angry, and—"

"Yes. I did." She climbed to her feet and began gathering up the remains of their Christmas tree picnic to take to the kitchen, to clean up so she could go to bed alone.

Gabriel rose behind her, disgruntled at himself as much as he was with her. He'd decorated the apartment on a whim because, no matter how much he tried to rationalize his way out of getting too close, he wanted to be there with her, and he wanted her to see it. See…what was too soon to say. Know that he knew how to make a home. He was husband material, not just parental partnership material, because that was the only thing he could think of to get this point across. Prove this by deeds. His mind was already made up about her, but she needed time and reassurance.

And he'd probably also done it because he didn't know what to tell her.

She clearly didn't want help with the dishes, so Gabriel went to pick up the boxes of ornaments they hadn't hung on the tree yet, clearing up something of the mess. "I only know how to do this one way. I only know how to reason my way through steps to show you that you can trust me. You want promises, fine. I won't stay with you for the baby if—"

"Children. It'll be more than one in a few years if you truly see us being together forever," she cut in, turning back from the sink with a towel to dry her hands. "Because you want me. And I want you. Most of the time. You might be able to hold off, control whether you want me, or how much you want me, but I don't work that way. I don't want to rush you any more than I want you to rush me, but it would probably go a long way toward convincing me that you feel something for me besides attraction and affection if you *stopped* holding yourself back so much."

"What am I holding back?"

"I don't know. I know you take a year to come up with a half-sentence, you hold me back when I want to kiss you. The other day? That kiss was amazing, and I'm sure a lot of that was because you made me slow down enough to really appreciate it, but between your half-finished thoughts and your insane restraint levels, you can tell me you want me until you're out of breath, but it's only words." She tossed the towel on the counter, and as he stood between her and the stairs, she stepped to the side to go round him. "I'm going to bed."

She passed him, having every intention of continuing toward the stairs. Leave him down here with his perfect, glittery chest and his impermeable walls. Let him control the downstairs, she was going up.

She was almost past him when she felt the air stir as he reached for her, one large hand catching her by the back of the neck and the other arm swooping around her waist, spinning her toward him.

Alarm spiked in her belly, but it turned to delight as his mouth came down on hers, tearing from him a groan so loud she'd have thought him in pain. Like steel girders twisting and buckling under the pressure, the sound of Gabriel's control snapping.

Her feet, unprepared, tangled and she grabbed for his shoulders, relying on his strength and the vestiges of his control to keep her upright. It worked as long as she hung there, taking his ravenous kisses, his demanding tongue, his heat and need as she struggled to catch up.

Trying to get her footing, she pulled on his shoulders for support, and just to get closer, and shifted her feet around to find some balance that didn't rely on him, but one of her feet crossed his and he stumbled backward, pulling her with him.

The twinkling Christmas tree broke their fall, and the fall broke their kissing. Gabriel managed to twist them so that she landed on his chest with a grunt on the pillows and comforter they'd picnicked on earlier.

"Are you okay?" she gasped against his lips, lifting enough to look at him, but he only nodded and rolled them, grabbing the cotton-candy-pink fuzzy pajama bottoms and dragging them off her roughly, panties and all.

CHAPTER SEVEN

PENNY'S TOP FLEW off next, and even though she was naked from the waist down, as soon as Gabriel saw another of those strappy white tanks she liked to wear, as she'd worn in Schenectady, he actually moaned before lunging at her chest. Through the snug, stretchy fabric, he caught her nipple, and every inch of her body sparked.

This was what happened when Gabriel lost control? The material scraped over the stiff peak of her breast, hot and wet from his mouth, and left her too shocked to do anything but grab at his shoulders while his big body pressed her into the pillows.

He finally seemed to realize the tank was there, and let go of her long enough to shove the material up over her breasts, where he could get at the now insanely sensitive flesh.

One hand stroked downward, over her belly, to

land between her legs, cupping, warming with his palm, then pressing just firmly enough to part tender flesh and stroke her.

She should be touching him, the thought drifted through her mind. Getting those damned pants off him at least. But she'd never felt so wanted, and it overrode her senses, left her quaking, arching, gasping, full of involuntary movements and sounds. Uncontrolled, desperate, and stunned, she clung to him because her fingers wouldn't stop gripping his shoulders.

They weren't just words, thank the Ghost of Christmas Sexy-Time... He wanted her. He really, really wanted her.

Gabriel closed his eyes and kissed and nibbled up her chest, up the side of her neck, trying to wrest some control back before he accidentally hurt her, went too fast, got too rough.

The taste of her skin and the feel of her writhing made an urgent beast inside him roar to life, but seeing how deeply pink she'd grown and the wild, blank look in her eyes made it too hard to even try to hold back.

The mother of his child, the woman he *wanted* to marry. It wasn't just for the child, God help him.

Her slickness on his hand, the puffy swelling there, it was as long as he could wait. The denim of his jeans already pinched, he'd grown so desperate for her. Wrestling the fasteners open, he shoved the material down, but before he got where he needed to be if he was going to keep breathing, Penny seemed to regain enough of her senses to do something besides squirm and make those pleading little mewls that all but assured he'd never be able to go slowly with her again. She focused enough to grab his head and drag it to hers.

Still no words, but she made her need for his kisses known through a series of throaty cries that only stopped when he covered her mouth with his own, and angled his head to stroke his tongue deeply into her mouth.

But he needed to be inside more than just her mouth.

Condom. The word habit he'd drilled into himself years ago rolled through the fog of need that had become his mind, but there was enough functioning there to discard it. No need.

Self-control slipping, he gripped her hips just to stop her squirming long enough to slide in. First damned night, and he'd said they had to wait...

Looking at her, her swollen lips open for gasping breaths, and feeling her hot around him, it hadn't been like this before. It had been hot and sexy and, God, *fun*, but this ache driving him... he felt it in spiky jabs straight down to the arches of his feet.

"Gabriel?"

She whispered his name and he held himself still, eyes closed, trying to breathe, trying not to buck against her the way he knew would if he didn't get hold of himself.

"Give me a second..." He pulled words together from somewhere.

Something was wrong. Penny searched his pained features, took in the violence of the shaking that had taken hold of him, and began to come back to herself. Yes, something was wrong, and she had no idea what it was.

"Is it too much?" she asked, feeling the need to

soothe him, now that she had a second to think without drowning in sensation.

He nodded, eyes still clenched shut, breaths harsh, labored, fighting for something.

"Want me on top?"

The question hung there for several seconds before he nodded, pushed an arm under her back, and rolled them over.

It was her turn to slow them down, for him. Kiss his neck, kiss his face, stroke her hands over his magnificent, glittery chest as she sat up, straddling him.

When he finally opened his eyes again, the look he gave her was full of such longing she couldn't look away. Not even when his hands firmed on her hips, urging her to move. Not even when she grew jerky and uncoordinated from the sizzling jolts of pleasure that pulsed through her. Not even when he sat up, put his strong arms around her, and kissed her.

Not even when she reached that dizzying height and had to fight to keep her eyes open while every other muscle in her body seized and jerked. Or when she felt him pulsing inside her.

He laid them back down among the pillows,

hearts thundering, Christmas tree toppled nearby, and a fire beside them.

But the last thing she felt before she closed her eyes was the certainty that she loved this man.

Penny stretched in the big comforter, feeling the crisp cotton slide against her skin, then spiraled through the last things she remembered to decide what was going on.

In her bed. That was wrong. She'd gone to sleep downstairs. With Gabriel.

She didn't even need to look beside her to know he wasn't there. The room felt empty, like always. Just like last time.

She knuckled the sleep from her eyes and sat up, taking further inventory. She was still nude, wrapped in the blanket from downstairs, and she hadn't climbed the stairs swaddled in the thing.

The sinking in her middle set off her inner nausea warning system, but when the retching didn't follow, she made herself examine it. Pounding heart, heightened awareness of every inch of her skin, of the amplified sound of her breathing. More dread. And bigger, sharper than that.

Fear. That was fear…that something bad was

going on with Gabriel and she didn't know enough of how relationships should go to fix it. Or that it was something unfixable.

A look at the other side of the bed confirmed it: blankets entirely unrumpled. Once again, he hadn't wanted to sleep with her. And she didn't know what to do with that.

Right.

She took a breath and dragged herself out of bed. Find him, look for reasons to support this fear, and don't give in to it until there's a good reason to.

Go downstairs, and if he's just somewhere *else* asleep, kick him in the happy place.

Ignoring her shaking insides, she dressed and brushed her hair to look her most presentable, and headed downstairs.

The scent of bacon hit her first, and she found him at the range. To the right, the Christmas tree they'd toppled sat upright again, but looked a little worse for wear, as she was, all evidence of their love nest missing entirely.

Gabriel stood at the range, making breakfast, but at the first sound of her feet on the stairs, what had been hunger gnawing at his belly turned into a slow, uneasy roll.

"Hey," he called, looking over his shoulder at her, silently praying for another calm, easy breakfast together, but knew how useless that prayer was. He'd been downstairs since dawn, having slept in the guest room, fitfully.

With a knot in his gut he scanned her face. The anxious drawing of her mouth confirmed she was upset. That, and her complete lack of greeting in return.

Upset and calm, which made him as uneasy as she looked. Energetic, loud Penny he knew how to deal with, not this version with sad eyes that shot right through his guilt center.

At work he knew how to speak with her, mostly without things getting fraught. Here, he didn't know which way to step. Apologizing for leaving her, as he truly wanted to do, was the wrong move. Pretending nothing was wrong at least made clear he didn't want to talk about things.

"How are you feeling?"

Her shoulders popped up, and she looked him over in a way that increased the feeling of dread.

"You've already had your shower and fixed the tree."

Tree. Quasi-safe subject. As long as he didn't mention how it had got knocked down.

"It still needs ornaments, but no damage done. I thought we could do that after breakfast. Do you think you can handle bacon?"

He could tell by the look of utter bafflement that damage had been done between them. This was a mess. Last night shouldn't have happened, it had been too much too soon. It had changed things too much, too quickly, and he'd already been having a hard time figuring out what was going on. She'd said she wanted to take things slowly too...

"You carried me up to bed last night?"

"Thought it was better than sleeping on the floor."

She was feeling her way too, he could see it in the pauses. Normally she spoke quickly, her excited babbling actually one of the things he enjoyed most about being with her. These heavy pauses made it worse. Not just the lack of excitement, which was the wrong direction for them to be traveling, but the fact that she was so carefully weighing all her words before uttering them.

"Where did you sleep?"

"In my room." He turned off the burner and moved the pan of bacon back so that he could give her all his attention.

"You didn't want to sleep with me?"

Still working through it. He should jump to the explanation, not leave her feeling her way. Wiping his hands, he went to stand across the island counter from her, where she'd eased onto a stool.

He kept his voice gentle and looked her in the eye, though she was having trouble maintaining eye contact with him, which ratcheted up the urge to reach for her. "We were taking things slowly, and then we didn't take things slowly. I was trying to put us back on course."

"What course?"

"Slower, more meaningful intimacy. You wanted it to flow naturally."

She gestured with one hand toward the fireplace, and finally looked him in the eye again. "Sleeping beside me in the bed is more intimate than *that* was?"

"It is, or you wouldn't be upset now."

"I'm upset because I went to sleep in your arms and woke up alone in a different room on a different floor of my home…" She stopped abruptly, holding up her hands and breathing so deeply that dread started to twist at him. Was she going to cry? Not sleeping beside her, not waking up tangled in her sheets with her, was supposed to make this easier.

"We have to stop getting swept up in the physical stuff."

"Why?"

"Because that's just the way it is. Don't you think about how messy this can get if we're not clear and careful about what we're doing?"

"I thought we agreed that this was a relationship."

"We did, and we have very different ideas about relationships and needs. The surest way to make this end in a formal custody battle is to be sloppy and irresponsible now."

Her fists squeezed and released, flexing with the tension she had rolling off her.

"Fine. Rule Number One: if you sleep with a woman, the civil thing to do is wake her up before you leave her."

"Fine."

"Rule Number Two: I'm feeling better, and going back in the air tomorrow."

"That's not a rule." Again it was turning into a fight. "And you're not well enough. You don't even know if it will manifest once you're in the air, like motion sickness."

"I guess we'll find out." She stood up and moved into the kitchen, no longer looking at him, like that could switch off the conversation as easily as she switched on the kettle.

"Penny…"

She rubbed both hands over her face, then waved a hand, like she was trying to dispel the tension. "Tomorrow, at work, if I feel bad I'll go home."

A concession. A compromise of sorts. Except… "You won't. You never admit you're sick until you're forced to."

"I called off the other day."

He took a breath and then nodded. She had him there. "And you know if you don't, I'll send you home."

"I know it if anyone knows it," she muttered,

grabbing the cider from the fridge and pouring it into a mug before sticking it in the microwave.

Touching her always helped, she took comfort in it as much as he did when they were at an impasse. He stepped over to her, but didn't touch her until she looked up at him.

Not moving away from him. Gabriel took that as permission, and brushed his hand over her hair and pressed his lips to her forehead.

She leaned in for the barest second, then pulled back. "Don't."

"Don't what?"

"Don't kiss my head."

Head kissing was innocuous. "Why?"

"It makes me feel like you really care."

"I do care."

"Kind of. You proved wanting me, the sexual connection. But you didn't want to sleep with me. That's twice now. First, you wanted to sleep in the same bed as me, and then you left in the night. Then last night I went to sleep with you, after all that, and you left again. Actually, you took me somewhere else and left me there."

"That's stretching what happened. I took you to your bed, not to Dubuque."

"You said it was because of not wanting too much intimacy. That's all I'm asking for. Because as much as you hate that I won't just marry you, I'm the one who keeps ending up being rejected by you. Let's just leave it at that. I won't ask you to sleep in the bed with me, you don't kiss my head like I'm some sweet thing you can't get enough of. Because clearly I'm not."

Denials were rushing to his lips as soon as the words began to make sense to him, but he clamped his mouth shut. She believed that. The only thing clear to him was that his attempt to reset the situation had made things worse, not better.

The next morning was gray and frigid. Overnight, rain had arrived in the city, and then the temperature dropped. She could tell how nasty it was by the coating of ice on her bedroom windows.

A day for thermals beneath her flight suit. Maybe two layers. And two pairs of socks.

Had Gabriel thought to bring a set with him for their temporary trial run? She'd been ignoring the *temporary* part of the arrangement before yesterday, but it truly felt temporary today. Yes, she'd wanted to let things unfold naturally, but nothing, prior to waking up alone, had felt unnatural. She couldn't decide if he was doing this on purpose, or if he truly thought he was helping their situation, and her relationship IQ was practically nil.

Snatching a second set of thermals from her bureau, she stuffed them into the messenger bag she preferred to handbags, then dragged on baggy jeans and sweater to tide her over until she got to the hospital and a fresh, clean flight suit. She'd decide on the commute if she needed the second set, though hers would never fit him anyway.

"Pen?" he called from downstairs, sounding as tense as she'd felt since yesterday.

It was that tension more than anything else that prompted her to hurry. Snatching a brush and hairband on the way out, she went to meet him.

He stood by the door, ready to go, keys and bag in hand. "Everything okay?"

Nope.

"I'm not feeling sick."

He had his keys out, he could lock it up. She

stepped on out and went to ring for the elevator, and ignored a disgruntled sigh behind her.

They lapsed into silence for the whole ride to the hospital, with him tucking his nose into his phone and her braiding her hair.

In the locker room, which she realized she hadn't seen him in for weeks, she noted a set of thermals when he changed into his flight suit, and she added her second set because she got colder than he did. But the silence was like a hulking thing in the room with them.

"I'm going to get the pre-flight done."

"I'll come with you."

She knew she winced when he looked at her in a way that said he'd seen it.

With one step, he blocked her exit from the otherwise empty locker room. "We have to get it together. It was a fight. Or a disagreement, or a whatever you want to call it, not the end of the world. If you can't be alone with me in the chopper, we're in serious trouble."

"I can be alone with you in the chopper."

"You wouldn't stay in a room with me yesterday."

"You *hurt* me. Do you get that?"

Just coming out with it seemed to make the situation register with him, she saw it in the way his jaw clenched and he looked away briefly before nodding and looking back to her. One simple acknowledgment shifted what had been feeling like blame to a more neutral footing.

"I know." He said the words she needed to hear, shoving his hands into the pockets of his suit with stiff arms that pulled at the material and showed his discomfort. "I didn't mean to. I'm sorry, and I should've said it yesterday."

An apology was the last thing she'd expected. Acknowledgment would've been enough to satisfy her, but the gruffly spoken apology left her feeling more vulnerable than admitting he'd hurt her. "I get it. It's hard to talk about this stuff, especially if you don't trust me to handle it right."

His silence confirmed the mistrust still there.

"I need to go do the pre-flight before we get any calls. The way things are going out there, you know as soon as we're on duty, calls are coming," she said, letting him off the hook, if for no other reason than because she needed her wits about her if she was going to get through her first day back, without him thinking that she was incapable of performing her duties.

He nodded again, but didn't immediately move out of the doorway. A long silence followed, when he clearly wrestled with whether to say something else, then apparently decided against it as he moved out of the way, then fell into step behind her as she hit the stairs for the roof.

The less he talked, the more certain she got that this wasn't going to work. She should just go to the lawyer tomorrow and have documents started to acknowledge Gabriel as father and begin a joint custody arrangement. It couldn't hurt, and at this point it might be the only thing to save *them*.

CHAPTER EIGHT

As soon as his butt hit the seat, Gabriel switched on the radio. Seconds later, a call came from Dispatch for them.

While Penny went through the pre-flight as fast as she could, he answered.

"I know you're not on shift for another ten, but are you ready to fly yet? Massive pileup on the turnpike at the tunnel toll gates. They're calling in all flight crews."

Gabriel looked at her for confirmation they were ready.

She nodded. "Thirty to flight."

"We're go in thirty."

Grabbing her headset, Penny put it on, buckled in, and he did the same. After she'd checked a couple more things, they lifted off.

"Told you it'd be a busy morning," she said into the comm, "but we're about ten minutes away. I hope they have some ground crews doing triage."

He knew what she was doing, she was trying to make things easier between them, and he appreciated it. Since yesterday morning Penny didn't feel quite so much like the stumbling block to their relationship. He could see she was trying, and the extent of her honesty on any situation cleared up his confusion. He didn't trust her, she said it again and again, but he was starting to wonder if it was her he didn't trust. He trusted her on the job, at least when she wasn't ill as she claimed to not be today, but nothing in their history said he couldn't trust her. Maybe he didn't trust himself.

But he could trust their working relationship, so he leaned on it now.

"Ice and morning rush hour are always bad. I'm going to bet we've got some broken bones, head trauma, maybe stress-induced cardiac events." With any other partner Gabriel wouldn't gamble on the injuries they'd find on accident scenes, it could come off as callous, but no money was ever involved. It had actually turned into a teaching method between them, or more for Penny. She didn't have medical school under her belt, but she had extremely good instincts, and the more she learned, the better at her job she got. She'd already gotten to the point where she could anticipate his needs at least as well as any nurse he'd ever worked with in the ER.

"I'm gonna bet on…some kind of bashing chest injury. Pneumothorax. Hemothorax. Something like that. Flail chest, maybe. Breathing difficulties. Did you double-check inventory on your last shift? What do I need to grab when we jump?"

He went through a list of what he'd grab, confirmed his freshly stocked bag, and told her to grab the board and he'd grab oxygen then run ahead.

"Two minutes," she announced, and then groaned into the headset in a way that set him instantly alert.

"What is it? Are you sick?"

"Look down there." She nodded ahead to the accident scene they were still a good mile away from. Headlights and taillights pointed in all different directions, and there was an overturned tractor trailer blocking two lanes.

"Where are you going to set down?"

"Back of the semi, there's a clear space where cars can't get until that thing is moved…"

"Okay." He unbuckled and climbed into the back to grab his bag and a couple of items, assuming she wasn't ill since she hadn't said, and didn't look it, then held on as she touched down.

The chopper bounced a little and then actually slid, which was new.

"Are we sliding?" he shouted over his shoulder.

"For about a second. Careful when you climb out."

"You too." He looked at the board, considering if it'd be too much for her to carry with the slick conditions, then grabbed the oxygen and went ahead with his original plan.

That was another reason he didn't want her flying right now, because he factored her well-being into every decision, and there wasn't time for that on the ground.

He wrenched open the door and eased out then, with the bags on one shoulder and oxygen on the other, began slipping his way around the semi, and had to grab the hulking metal beast twice to keep from falling down.

Just on the other side of it, one of the cops organizing the scene met him and directed him to his patient's vehicle, an upside-down rust-colored SUV with glass shattered all around.

"My pilot is coming with the board—direct her."

He didn't worry that she'd see the wreck, but there were at least fifteen cars he could see with massive damage and no doubt casualties, and he needed her to find *him*.

He hurried along a path through the wrecks that had been obviously hand-salted, and which provided him better traction. Another NJSP trooper had crawled in through the passenger window. Gabriel could only see legs and feet and so rounded the vehicle to gain access from the other side.

"I'm Dr. Jackson," he said immediately as he looked inside. On the roof, lying over a shattered sun roof, a man lay on his back, white button-down shirt saturated with blood and a tire iron sticking out of his chest.

The officer sat upright, wedged between the seats so she could apply pressure.

"We didn't take it out," she said immediately, "but he's still bleeding. I applied pressure as best I could…"

"Okay, get out and when my partner gets here, direct her in that side," he ordered, and lifted up so he could better examine his patient, almost wishing the man was unconscious. "What's your name?"

"Darren." He said the short first name, and Gabriel could tell he was having trouble breathing. Damn if Penny hadn't nailed it. She hadn't called an open pneumothorax, but she'd called chest damage and difficulty breathing.

"I'm going to get you to Manhattan Mercy, Darren. As soon as I can." He gloved and pulled the compress away from the base of the wound, doing his best not to move the iron, but even a slight touch caused more pain. "I'm sorry about that. I'm trying to decide if we can pull it out."

"I wish you would."

Penny appeared at the other window and crawled in, dragging another bag with her and pulling out oxygen to hook up to the bottle he'd carried.

"His name is Darren." Gabriel filled her in, handing her the bottle. "He needs a line and he needs morphine."

Judging by the usual length of a tire iron,

Gabriel estimated that Darren had about four inches of metal jammed into his ribs. The difficulty breathing could be because of the pain—the more it hurt to breathe, the more shallowly people breathed.

Penny didn't waste any time. She tied off his arm and threaded in a catheter before Gabriel could listen to his chest to decide whether to pull out the iron.

"If we lay the seats down, we can get probably get him out the hatchback," she said, flushing the line. "Darren, I'm going to give you something for pain, and you're going to go to sleep. We're going to take you by air to the hospital, so you will be in the hands of a surgeon within a quarter-hour, okay?"

He nodded, and Penny injected the morphine, flushed the line again, and hooked up a saline drip. Before she was done, Darren was unconscious and Gabriel could listen to natural, painless breathing.

"His lungs are wet," he muttered to Penny. "Okay, lay the seat down there, I'll get mine and go around the back to get the hatchback and pass in the backboard."

She got done first, and he heard her on her radio. "Wet lungs, tire iron protruding. I don't know if we're going to tube him, but he's breathing on his own for now. If we can't get him out of the vehicle with the iron in, we might have to pull it. He doesn't have time to wait for them to cut the doors off."

He hadn't directed her to say that, but she was right. It really was a shame that she hadn't had the patience for medical school.

With the seats were laid back and the hatchback opened, and they managed to get Darren out of the overturned car. As soon as they had cleared it, Penny hung the saline on Gabriel's shoulder as usual, and they moved as swiftly as they could for the chopper.

While they'd been in the vehicle, someone had thrown down what looked like cat litter on the ice, and around the jack-knifed truck to the chopper, so their path was easier. Barely more than a minute after they'd loaded the stretcher, Penny had them in the air.

The doorbell had Penny jolting awake on the sofa where she'd fallen asleep. It took her several seconds to ground herself and remember what was going on. Miranda. Visit. Right.

She scrambled upright and smoothed her hands over her hair, praying it wasn't sticking up like crazy. Gabriel had gone out to do Christmas shopping because she'd practically shoved him out the door earlier. This seemed like the kind of visit to not have your significantly strange other hanging around for.

Flinging the door open, she put on her best smile, and waved Miranda in.

"Oh, wow, did you do all this or hire someone?" her sister asked after the hug of welcome, leaving Penny to close the door. "Or is that even a service you can hire, like a Christmas interior decorator?"

Miranda hadn't grown up the same way Penny had, something that Penny often forgot. They'd had Miranda in the family for about half of her life now, long enough for everything to normalize to the point that it felt as if she'd always been there. The only way Miranda was any different from her brothers, aside from being female, was not having had to suffer through the sickness of the baby sister ruining fun things.

"You actually can, but I didn't hire anyone. I bought all the stuff, intending to put it up, but I came home from my shift on the floor the other day and Gabriel had put it all up." Nice lead-in. She was almost proud for just slipping that in there.

"Gabriel Jackson? Your partner? Why?"

"I guess he was being sweet," Penny said, something she'd been quietly smiling about every time she'd looked at the twinkling lights, even while things had been tense between them. "He'd just moved in, which we haven't told anyone yet, and he still has his place for now but, yeah. He's living here. For now. But it's still cone-of-silence stuff because it's a trial run and we're not doing so well with it. Have…things to figure out."

Miranda knew Penny's history, so she looked suitably surprised by the news. "What things do you have to figure out?"

She ushered Miranda to the kitchen and put on the kettle. It was time for tea and another antiemetic. And the part of the conversation she wasn't exactly looking forward to.

"Oh, mostly how to be together without messing everything up. We've got reasons to try and figure it out."

Miranda draped her coat and bag over one stool and sat at the other, amusement in her voice. "You mean like you love him?"

That part of the conversation Penny was not ready for. "Reasons like… I'm pregnant."

Time for Miranda's second shock in as many minutes. "Uh, congratulations?"

Penny nodded, and after getting the mugs ready for when the water was hot, she went to stand on Gabriel's side of the island—in the kitchen, facing her sister on her own usual stool. "Thank you. It is… It's good news. I do want the baby, and so does he, so that's good news. But…um…boy, you know, in my head I didn't just go storming right into the heart of this conversation as soon as you walked through the door."

"There's more to the conversation than you're living with someone and pregnant?"

"Yeah." Penny sighed, leaning her elbows on the counter because if she put her hands on the polished marble, she'd start tapping or fidgeting. "I know we don't talk about, you know, Dad and your mom, and pretty much all that, but even knowing that you're bound for Spain and marriage and duchesshood…duchessdom?… I was a little worried that my deciding to be a single mother could be uncomfortable for you. And I didn't want you to find out from anyone else, or in front of anyone else, which is why I shoved Gabriel out the door about half an hour ago. You can yell at me if you feel…you know, moved to yell at me."

"But you said Gabriel moved in."

"Well, yeah, temporarily. Because we're both hot for each other and too stupid to know how to have a relationship. I'm not ready for marriage, and neither is he, no matter if he's willing to sacrifice himself at the altar for the baby. He's got a bad marriage in his past, and I've got Mom and Dad. I'm pretty much in awe that any of us, let alone all you guys, want to get married. It's fine for you, I mean if you're happy with it, which I assume you are on account of saying yes… I'm just not, which isn't just about them. We're not navigating the obstacles very well."

Miranda nodded like she understood, and Penny didn't explain further. "But you want to be with him?"

"I don't know what I want." She looked at the sparkling tree, then back at Miranda. "No, that's not right. I know I don't want a husband to try and control me, stifle my freedom, grow to hate me, but stay together because of pride and obligation, any of that. But I want to be with him, at least when he's not being an idiot."

She took a moment from her breakdown to pour the hot cider into cups, then followed with the hot water, teabags and cinnamon sticks. Then placed one in front of her sister and went to join her on another stool. "How did you get there? Or were you always hoping to get married?"

"Not always." Miranda answered that first, and then stirred the tea with the cinnamon stick, watching the mug for a long moment. "It's okay, I'm sorry to know that you're struggling, wish I had some advice. We had some obstacles too, but I guess sometimes you have to decide it's worth letting go and just trying. Or that's what it was for us."

"Letting go of what?"

Miranda shrugged. "Fear? Protecting yourself?"

"Oh, is that all?" Penny lifted her mug and took a drink, chuckling over the warm liquid.

"What are you afraid of?"

"Losing myself." The words flew from Penny's mouth before she thought them through, then she shook her head. "That's not exactly it. I'm apparently riddled with issues, but the truth is that I'm willing to try, which is more than I ever thought I would be. It just doesn't seem like he really is willing to try. He has this strange yo-yo thing going on. Sometimes he is so sweet it just about kills me, and then, usually right after he's been amazing, he shoves me so far away that I end up in another room, in another city, on another planet."

Miranda took her hand, and Penny admired the stunning ring on her finger and stopped this pity party.

"Mateo picked a good ring."

It was easy to go with a subject change when there was nothing helpful to say, or when the subject turned to happier news. "It's gorgeous, isn't it?"

"I'd wear it. I mean, not to marry Matteo, obviously. I meant I'd wear it and I hardly ever wear jewelry. So you know I like it." Penny blathered out a bunch of stupid words, grunted at herself and took a sip of her tea. "When's the wedding? Do I need another dress fitting? Because if it's not soon, I'm going to be hard to fit. I know that I'm not going to have a big ole belly by Charles and Grace's wedding, that's right around the corner. The other day when we were doing the dress fitting, that was all that was going through my mind. Not that you don't deserve a big fairy-tale wedding. If anyone does, it's you. Flowers and titles, and all the love. And I'm babbling again."

Soon they were talking all things wedding, from the beautiful dresses Grace had chosen for them and her maid of honor, Dr. Helena Tate, to speculation about when their cousin Jude and Dr. Sarah Grayson were heading for the altar. Penny would admit feeling a little envious about Miranda's coming move to Spain. Maybe next year Penny could take her baby to Spain for Christmas, spend it there if Gabriel wasn't here.

She took another drink of the tea, mostly to mask how her throat had closed up and her eyes watered, and she found herself looking at the single present under her Christmas tree. The gift she'd picked up for Gabriel yesterday and slipped under the tree before he'd gotten home from work.

The kicker of their relationship, and the part of her parents' marriage Penny didn't want to think about, was knowing it was lopsided. She loved him, but he didn't love her, and she didn't know if that also mirrored her parents' relationship. She'd rather think that at this late hour in their union they hated one another equally. It'd be even worse if one of them was still in love, still suffering.

The gift she'd put under the tree was supposed to show Gabe she still planned on him being there when Christmas finally rolled around in a couple of weeks. Sure, she'd gotten a kiss for it—not on the head—and he'd then taken the opportunity to debate whether it was better to open presents on Christmas Eve or Christmas Day, but things were still tense. She couldn't tell if he'd picked up on the subtext of her only gift purchase so far.

His wife had left without warning, though, so maybe she'd have left a gift for him just to maintain the fantasy of a happy marriage. Or maybe she'd been fooling herself and had then had just

206   THE RESCUE DOC'S CHRISTMAS MIRACLE

snapped one day and gone. All Penny had was Gabriel's words, and he'd been so hurt by it all, she couldn't really count on him having seen it clearly.

"Penny?"

"Sorry, I heard you. It's going to be a month of weddings with Charles's coming up, and you probably before the new year." She heard that much at least and, goodness, she had to pay better attention. She'd invited Miranda here to talk about *her* wedding and shining future, not Perilous Penny's. "Forgive me. I invited you over and I'm terrible company."

"It's okay. Do you want to call him?"

"No. He'll be back in…" Penny looked at the clock "…forty-five minutes, or about that. And considering how punctual he is, probably forty-four minutes."

"Should I be gone before he gets here?"

"Only if you want to flee. If you do, you have forty-three minutes to tell me how to fix this first, because you've obviously got your life together better than I do."

CHAPTER NINE

"GROUNDED," GABRIEL REPEATED, sitting on the bench in front of his locker to tug his boots off and change out of his flight suit, more for Penny than himself. Twice in one week Old Man Winter had invited himself to the city, and while it was possible to fly when the roads were slick, it was something else to fly when the snow fell this heavily.

Penny sat a couple feet down the bench from him, attention focused on her phone, but he knew she'd heard him by the pinching and vigorous pink shade of her lips, still angry that the decision had been made without her. "I'm looking at the radar, and there are gaps in the front. We will probably be able to take runs here and there, just not right now."

"Flying requires visibility." He cringed inwardly at himself. Even to his ears it sounded like he was talking down to her, because he was trying to soften the conflict, where he'd have just been direct before and let her be angry. So much for maintaining their working relationship.

"I know, I'm the pilot. When there are gaps in the cells, I'll be able to see for short runs."

He shook his head, but knew he wasn't going to be able to argue her out of hanging out and hoping. It was the same frustrating battle as sending her home when she was sick. "You're saying you're not going to go to the floor and help out?"

"Storms don't make people not need our services. We're Rescue, we're supposed to be focused on rescuing people whenever we can. They can't get treatment at a hospital if they can't get to a hospital. And the roads..."

"They're terrible, I know." He could agree with her on that part. Things were still tense between them, and every conversation felt like something that could knock them out of the air. "You really hate working on the floor that much?"

"I hate feeling confined. And I do when I'm down there. You might end up doing something exciting, but I usually end up babysitting." The word *babysitting* made her face squinch up, and she puffed. "I think it's time to stop using that word for that, it's increasingly looking like that will be my whole existence in a few months."

"What does that mean?"

"It means I'm not going to be able to do anything but take care of the baby. That sounds selfish, I know. It's not a worry for you because you're not on the verge of being shelved. I know I've had a rough start with the pregnancy, but I feel like other people are taking my choices left and right. Like you telling me to just go home now."

"It's just a better use of your time. Stay here if you want to." He could concentrate on his job better if she went home and didn't hang around the hospital seething because she couldn't do what she wanted or fretting about the people she couldn't help. One boot off, he rose to go peek at her phone and the radar she was currently refreshing. A continuous line of pale blue stretched from New York to West Virginia, and was blowing in such a way that they'd get every mile of that stripe of storms covering several states. "Look at that. You'll be less bored at home."

"There are pockets of flurries, especially here

for the next three-ish hours. Then it'll get heavy and stay heavy, but there's people we can help before it gets too bad."

Penny felt her hackles rising again. She knew that Gabriel was being sensible, rational even, but she listened to her gut, and her gut said this wasn't how her day was going to go. "Haven't you ever just felt like something was going to happen, and you want to be there for it?"

"Are you saying you have some kind of inkling you're going to go out there?" he asked, his eyes narrowing a touch, just enough for her to know he wasn't getting it.

What could she say? If she said yes, he'd have a fit and try to force her to go home. "I'm saying I feel like I have something to do today here, not at home. Maybe it's just being with Dispatch in case they need another hand. I don't know, but I'm not going home yet. Even if Dispatch doesn't need help, I can perform some maintenance on the chopper and make sure it's stocked better. I've noticed the supplies haven't been kept up as much as I like while I was gone."

"I'm not going to win this one, am I?"

"I'm pretty sure you have won. You and Charles conspired to entirely shut down flights for the day and I got no input in that. You grounded us. That means you did win. You just aren't winning the ordering Penny home conversation too." Penny tried to soften it with a smile, but she wasn't feeling very smiley.

He shook his head and crammed his boot back on, no longer changing out of his flight suit. "Call me if you get a window and permission to fly."

Fifteen minutes later, Penny was in the chopper with her tumbler of hot apple tea, powering everything up. She stuck her phone into the mount on the dash so she could keep the radar up and running, and the band radio set to listen, then went back to the rear to start her inventory.

She half listened to the radio chatter, just enough to hear her name or their unit number, and to make out the different kinds of calls going out. Bad fall at a museum. The place had slippery steps, and an injured patron.

All their arguments seemed to shadow the marriage argument, even when they had nothing to do with it.

He and Charles agreed there would be no flying, so she was grounded. He hadn't orchestrated it, but she was pregnant, which was kind of like being grounded when it came to doing things she wanted to do. And those were the two unchangeable positions that put her at a starting disadvantage.

"Cardiac arrest at Fifty-Ninth."

He wanted her to go home, and he wanted her to marry him. She'd said no going home, and that she'd work on something else, and she'd also said no to marriage, but she'd work on a relationship.

And they were both unsettled and unhappy.

"ETA Unit 377?"

"ETA Unit 410?"

Maybe she should just marry him. Maybe having that stability would calm him down, nothing else she'd done seemed to. At least he'd sleep in the same bed with her, she could reasonably demand he hug her or comfort her whenever she wanted. But that was part of the problem—she wanted to be fine on her own, without needing that comfort from him. And he seemed to feel more comfortable himself when he was doing something tangible for her.

"ETA Unit 219?"

If she didn't marry him, she might end up having this baby alone. Sure, he'd still be around to be a father, he'd made that completely clear, but she could end up forced to give birth on her own because having Mom there would stress her out, and Miranda was going to be in Spain by then.

She stopped counting and shuffling inventory to look at the radio in the front, and listened to units calling in left and right about the delays, the traffic, and one who was just stuck.

"We're sending a wrecker, 410."

Penny stashed what she'd counted out into her go-bag, and went to check her radar again.

"Any units available? Fire and ambulance needed."

The snow was falling lighter than it had been. Granted, the air had that strange, bluish, foggy quality over the city because of the falling snow, but she could see through it. She could see the roof of the building at the end of the block, which wasn't wonderful but it was something.

"What do you have, Dispatch?"

"Davenport?"

"Yes. Is everyone stranded?"

"It's a mess out there. We've got all units out and are trying to get NYPD to take this call."

"What's going on?"

"Woman in labor, trapped in an elevator."

Her stomach bottomed out and she grabbed the phone to look at the radar. There was a hole. She might not be able to make it *back* to the hospital with the woman, but she could get there. Be there, provide support, and wait for the next ground crew to arrive and take over.

When she'd been so sick, Gabriel showing up and making things better had been like a miracle to her when she had only been vomiting like crazy, not trying to give birth, alone, in a busted elevator.

"What's the address? Is it close enough to go on foot?"

She couldn't just leave her there.

There was a pause, then the answer, and confirmation that she couldn't get there by foot in the snow in less than an hour, even at a run.

She looked at the radar again. Oh, Gabriel would be angry. Charles would be angry. Everyone would be angry, except for the woman and her family. At the least the woman wouldn't be alone, like *she* might still end up.

She could make it there, she knew she could. And then she'd just have to leave the chopper until the storm passed, and come back with the ground crew.

Three switches got the chopper started. She waited until she'd lifted off to call in and let them know she was going.

"Dr. Jackson?" Gabriel turned at the sound of his name from the doorway to see Dr. Miranda Davenport standing there.

"Yes?"

"I'm sorry to interrupt, Dispatch needs you. It's Penny..."

He frowned over his shoulder at Miranda, instantly on alert. Penny wanted to go up. "I'll be right there. We were just finishing up."

It just took a minute to explain the testing he'd ordered to his patient and excuse himself to call upstairs, and about fifteen seconds for his blood pressure shoot into the stratosphere.

Penny had gone out without him. She'd gone out in the storm.

Miranda was at his heels so that when he
turned, ready to hit the stairs and get to Dispatch, he nearly ran her over.

"She went out in the snow?"

A nod was all he had time for.

Ninety seconds later he stood in the Dispatch
office, radio open after having called her as
calmly as he could, far calmer than his pounding heart wanted.

"I need to do this. I'm almost there," she called
back through the radio. "She needs help, Gabe."

Children were always one of Penny's triggers.
She'd do anything to get to a child in distress.
He'd seen her cow a vicious dog that had stood
between them and a child once. Logically, he
knew this about her, and she'd been that way as
long as he'd known her, long before she'd had her
maternal instincts kick into overdrive.

"Ground crews are going to help her. Come
back."

"They're at least twenty minutes behind me,
and I'm closer to the building than I am to Mercy
now. Stop distracting me. I'm flying in snow, I
need to concentrate."

She switched off and it felt so final that a

swell of premature grief robbed him of words. Swamped with helplessness, rage took control and sent the radio flying into the cinderblock walls of the Dispatch room. It struck hard, then crashed to the floor to clatter across the polished tile, but did little for his state of mind. It was less satisfying to smash unsmashable things against a wall—their radios were built to survive being dropped several stories.

And she was speaking the truth. Distracting her would put her into more danger. All he could do right now was wait.

She'd all but declared earlier that she was going to go out on her own, her gut having told her she was needed today somewhere. Heaven help him, he could barely reason with her under the best circumstances, she listened to her emotions first, reason second. His stomach lurched and he went to pick up the radio to make sure it was on, that he could hear if she called for help.

While waiting, he peppered the staff manning the radio with questions about where the call had come from, then mapped the address. Five minutes of flight, six tops. He looked at the clock. They'd called him as soon as she'd called saying she'd taken off, and he'd run from Emergency to the top of the tower after finishing with his patient, which had taken about three minutes total. Add another minute on the radio with her.

He'd give her two minutes to call in before he lost his mind.

Unable to hold still, he paced the small room until asked to sit. People were there. People had seen him throwing the radio. Would hear everything.

And he didn't give a damn anymore.

Heartbeats thundered in his ears, so loud he wasn't sure he'd hear the radio if she called. It was more that and the fact that he might be having a heart attack that made him sit.

This felt just the same. It wasn't the same, but it felt it. When Nila had gone, he hadn't been able to say anything to change her mind then either. But this was worse. If this was the last time he saw Penny, it wouldn't be by choice. It wouldn't be because she'd remarried and had children with another man, the family she hadn't wanted with him only two years earlier.

He could lose the baby if she crashed. He could lose *her*.

Seconds after he sat, the radio beeped and he heard her.

"I'm down."

He felt eyes on him, but closed his eyes to block them out. Help her. She'd need help.

She was down now, she was safe. Ground crew would come soon.

"What equipment are you taking?" he asked, and waited, willing his voice to be steady and calm.

"Extra blankets. IV, saline. First-aid basics. Rope."

She sounded confident, more than him at least.

"Rope?"

Dammit, he'd forgotten the elevator. "Listen to me, Penny. Do not rappel more than two floors. The shorter the better. If she's between two floors, go to the one directly above it. As close as you can get."

Problem was, he didn't know if the elevator doors on every floor could be forced open. He didn't know why this elevator was stuck. He didn't know anything.

"I'll call building security and tell them to meet

you and help. Take a scalpel and clamps. You'll need them."

"Scalpel?" The first hint of hesitation. She didn't treat so much as triage usually.

"It might become necessary. You want to be prepared."

"Yes. Right. Scalpel."

She confirmed with a number from the small selection they had on the chopper.

"Have you delivered a baby before?"

"No…"

He rubbed between his eyes, trying to stop the tension headache he felt coming. "Have you been at a birth before?"

"Yes. I had some training, but I might need a refresher."

Chopper paramedics were usually involved with accidents, not births. If there was trouble, she'd be in over her head.

"What about oxygen?" she asked, breaking into his thoughts. "Should I take the small tank and masks?"

"Yes. And call me the minute you get into the elevator. I'll talk you through it."

As soon as he stopped talking, he remembered

another thing and shouted into the radio. "Stethoscope! Take a stethoscope…"

"Dr. Jackson, do you need some help?" one of the dispatchers asked, and he thought a moment and nodded.

"I need an ETA on the crews heading for the building. How are they doing?"

Having them there helped, he'd get as organized as he could. Pulling out his cellphone, he had the other dispatcher read him the number for building security and called to do what he'd promised, but messed up the number three times because of shaking hands.

If he believed in Christmas miracles, he could use one right now. Smooth, easy delivery. Healthy mom and baby. Crew arriving before the action started. That would be the best, if they got into the elevator or got it moving with plenty of time to get them all to the hospital before she had to push or lose it.

Juggling his cell and radio was all he could do, and pray, and the last might be a bad idea until he could control his emotions or he'd just end up screaming at God.

* * *

Penny stuffed two large bags with supplies, slung them both ways across her torso, threw the coil of rope over one shoulder, shoved the radio into her pocket, and grabbed the backboard.

She should've asked Gabriel to have them meet her on the roof to haul equipment, she'd be exhausted before she got into the shaft at this rate.

No. Now was not the time for defeatist thinking. She could do this. She'd flown in the snow, landed successfully. And she'd help that woman and baby. Every ounce of her exhaustion tonight would be righteous and hard-won. She'd picked rescue as a career for just this kind of reason.

As needy as she'd been when she'd been vomiting everywhere, Gabriel's arrival couldn't have been more heaven sent if the actual Angel Gabriel had popped into her apartment in her time of need. And she hadn't even been trying to push a baby out of her body in a freaking elevator shaft at the time.

She scooted through the roof access door and inside. A moment to stomp the snow from her boots, and she hit the stairs, bracing the backboard on her head and balancing with one hand so she could get the radio.

"Gabe."

"Are you there?"

"No. What floor? Did Security tell you what floor?"

"Twenty-five." His voice came through the radio, stilted, and measured. She could hear the effort it took him to speak evenly, and it curdled her stomach. "She's just below it."

"Okay." She knew it was a thirty-story building, relatively small by new building standards. Lucky she was close to the top if they had to carry her out. Lucky for *her*, too. Gabriel was too good a doctor and too good a man to leave her hanging on this, even when she could hear his frustration.

She switched off, stashed the radio again, and picked up the pace. Her weeks of stair-marathon conditioning helped and, even heavily laden, she made it there quickly. The elevator was just across from the stairs, and the security officer stood there, working on the doors as she stepped off.

"Do you need help?"

He looked back at her and nodded. "I've never done this before. I think I use this and put it here and turn, and that's supposed to unlock something, and then maybe we shove?"

He was as experienced with elevators as she was with birth.

"I've never done it before but, here, I'll take the crowbar and wedge it in, and as soon as you say, I'll pull it." She ditched her supplies on the floor and braced one foot against the side of the elevator entrance. As soon as he turned something she could only consider a lock and key mechanism, she pulled hard.

The doors popped and he got his hands in there to shove them open. Once it was done, she set the bar on the floor and bent over the edge to peer into the shaft. Maybe ten feet to the top of the box. She could probably dangle over the edge and just drop onto it, but even knowing there were locks to keep elevators from plummeting to the ground, she didn't want to just suddenly drop all her weight, along with the weight of her equipment, onto the elevator and tempt fate.

"Andrea?" She called the name that Dispatch had given her into the shaft, and when she heard a response, she introduced herself. "My name is Penny and I'm a paramedic from Manhattan Mercy air ambulance. There are still ground crews coming, but the roads are terrible. So I'm just going to come on down to you, okay?"

"Please hurry. I think my water broke."

The guard winced, but Penny managed to keep her face placid even if her guts were wincing in tandem with his face. She grabbed the rope and found a nearby pillar to secure it.

"Have you been on the phone with Dr. Jackson?" she asked the guard.

"Yes. I'm supposed to call when we get you in."

Of course he was. Gabriel would be doing all he could to help from his end, even if she was certain there'd be another showdown as soon as they got home later. She'd have rather had him with her, but there hadn't been time. The window would've passed before she could've gotten him to come up from Emergency, and he probably wouldn't have come anyway.

She slung her heavy bag around her again, the one with the oxygen and IV paraphernalia, and took the rope, saying to the guard before she stepped over the edge, "When I get down, I want you to toss me the second bag and hand me the board."

He nodded, and he looked so pale she'd have thought he was the father, but dutifully input numbers into his phone and got ready to hit Send.

It was only about ten feet down, but the rope made her feel more secure, even if she only had to rappel about seven feet before she put her foot down on the top of the elevator.

Which bounced when she stepped onto it.

"Penny?"

"It's okay, that's just me. I'll be right there. If you're feeling like you have to push, try not to… I don't know where you are yet."

And all she remembered from her training involved full dilation being needed before the pushing…but the urge to push often came earlier.

The guard lay on the floor above and stretched the board down, then, when it was still braced against the side of the shaft, dropped the softer bag of first-aid supplies onto it so it slid toward her. Then called down instructions on how to open the top hatch.

She threw the end of the rope through with her heavier bag tied to the end, then dropped in the light bag, and then realized she didn't know how to get the board through.

Dangit.

Planned badly... Assuming she was still a team, that she could slide in and have someone, Gabriel, hand it to her. She grabbed it, turned it diagonally so it would fit through, and then began to lower herself to her knees, and further, and further, until she was lying on her belly, hanging through the top, finally getting it to touch down so she could lever it to the side in a way that wouldn't hit her patient.

Her patient, who was lying on the floor, red faced and breathing heavily. Immediately, she got worried. The elevator still had lights, which was a blessing, but it meant she got to see how terrified Andrea looked, and the amount of pain she was in.

"Tell me how you're doing, Andrea. Have you been timing your contractions? What are you feeling?"

While waiting, she pulled back out of the elevator and climbed in feet first instead of head first.

"Pain," came the woman's one-word answer, and when Penny looked at her, she had rolled onto her side and was obviously trying to breathe through another contraction.

"Everything's going to be okay. You have me, and we have the complete focus of a doctor at the hospital." Which was when she rang Gabriel for help, confirming with the puddle on the floor that the water had gone. "Dr. Jackson, I'm in. She's… mid-contraction, and her water has broken."

Kneeling down, she pressed her fingertips to Andrea's neck and counted, then reported the elevated pulse.

He began asking questions, and as the intermediary she relayed answers and performed different checks. Getting the backboard down, she spread a blanket on it and then helped Andrea onto it, where she'd be a tiny bit more comfortable, but mostly because it would be easier for transport after help came. She rolled another blanket for a pillow before getting gloves on and following Gabriel's instructions to check dilation.

Confirmed: total.

Did she need oxygen?

Wouldn't hurt.

These were things she'd have done, but it was less scary to have someone else backing her on this one. Not because she didn't know the basics, but because his instructions were like a safety net, not for her but for Andrea and mini-Andrea, whenever it came out.

"I'm calling you and putting it on speaker. Get off the phone with anyone else. I can't keep pushing the button on this to talk if I'm gloved for sterility."

"Dialing you now."

She heard her phone ringing, got it out of her pocket, put it on speaker and set it to the side before tossing the radio onto the floor.

With his help, in between calls from the security guard above, they proceeded to deliver that baby.

Every single milestone felt like it was projected on a big screen in front of her and running in slow motion.

Crowning.

Someone called from above, a new voice. A new crew. They were going to try to open the door on floor twenty-four, it might be down enough to crawl through…

The baby spiraled further out, until there was a head visible.

Then there were shoulders, and Penny helped…

Then she was the first person to ever hold that baby.

"Lay the baby on the mother's stomach." Gabriel's voice came through the speaker.

The baby wasn't moving, wasn't crying. Every atom in her body seemed to seize, and it was all she could do to keep from screaming. Not breathing.

"I… Gabe…he's…uh…"

She heard a sound she knew was from the guard getting into the shaft above, someone was opening the doors to the floor below, and it sounded close.

"He'll breathe if you lay him there and get him warm. He's got a few minutes to start breathing on his own. There's oxygen still coming through the cord. It's okay. Get him warm."

She laid the baby on his mother's belly and began rubbing his back with another of her blankets, holding her breath until he started to squirm, and finally let loose a scream that made both her and Andrea start to cry.

"He sounds good." Gabriel's voice had gentled, and just hearing him made her heart soar. He'd be there when their baby was born, he'd be there, and he'd talk just like that, and he'd make this not scary, because it *was* scary. It was scary and not even the kind of scary thing she had always felt compelled to face down.

"He's beautiful," she confirmed, her voice croaking the words out as she wrapped the wonderfully screaming baby in a fresh, dry blanket.

Gabriel talked her through clamping the cord off, cutting it, and she finished by covering Andrea in the final blanket.

The elevator doors opened with about two feet of clearance onto the twenty-fourth floor.

"How are you guys doing in there?" a man's voice called through, and when she looked over, she could see his head.

"We're perfect. So is—"

"Bowie." Andrea filled in the baby's name and Penny smiled.

"She's on the board. Baby Bowie is wrapped up and ready too. If you two can take the bottom of the board and lower her down, I can strap them in and push her through the opening."

The paramedics and firemen—she now saw—

on the other side of the elevator all agreed and she began readying her patients for transport.

Which was when she saw the blood.

"Andrea?" She said the woman's name, and noticed the distinct fuzzy quality to her eyes when she opened them at hearing her name.

"Uh, she's bleeding. Gabe? She's bleeding."

"She'll be bleeding…"

"No. She's *bleeding*. There's a lot of blood."

She heard him swear and then picked up Bowie to hand him through the opening to one of the crew, then went back to her patient.

"She needs to get here, honey. I don't want… I don't know if she has… The ground…"

Time. She knew that sound in his voice. He was trying to tell her that Andrea needed to get to the hospital fast. She needed to fly, and he couldn't bring himself to say it.

"Would a line and saline help?"

"Yes."

"On it." Glad she'd passed the baby to the other crew, she dug into her bag and came out with tourniquet, a number twenty catheter, line, saline, a flush, and felt for a vein.

She didn't need to be talked through that. And

inside a minute she had a line in, flushed, and hung the saline from her shoulder so she could shove the board toward the opening and they could get her out of the elevator.

A paramedic she recognized helped her out as well, and she transferred the saline to his shoulder as she would've Gabriel.

"Saline buys a few minutes, but we need to get her to the hospital. How do you two feel about flying?"

Neither of them hesitated, just picked up the board. She took Bowie, held him close, left all her junk in the elevator, and gestured to a second elevator beside the malfunctioning one. "That one working?"

"Yes."

The button was pressed, and she went ahead, just like always, hitting the stairs, this time with Bowie in her arms, to get to the chopper and get it ready to take off while they got the patient to the roof.

Once there, she got the chopper started, rotors spinning, and watched from inside where she could keep the baby protected from the cold and wind. If they came out with their gurney, she'd have to dump theirs on the roof.

When they came out, they were still carrying the board, which left her free to settle in. She laid Bowie in the co-pilot's seat, opened the side door, then went to her seat. In a flash, she got the headset on, buckled in, and picked the baby up again while they loaded Andrea. It was when they opened the door again that she fully realized how strong the wind had grown.

Only when the doors were closed did she hand Bowie back to one of them, and skipped the radar. The snow, no longer falling as lightly as it had been when she'd made the flight out, swirled around them. It wasn't as heavy as it could be, but no way would she normally fly in these conditions. Truly, the wind was worse than the snow. She knew the skyline so well she could practically fly it blindfolded, but the wind added a wildcard she didn't want to consider. There was nothing she could do about the wind, and not going would mean Andrea died.

She took a breath and lifted off, calling through the headset to Gabriel that they were airborne, and updates as the paramedics relayed them to her. He'd need two teams on the roof, one for Bowie and the other for Bowie's mother.

It wasn't that far.

She'd be able to see the lights, and she knew the way well enough to fill in any gray areas.

They'd be okay. She wouldn't panic and they'd all be okay. Gabriel would help them once she got them there.

They'd be okay…

CHAPTER TEN

LONGER EVEN THAN the three minutes he'd waited to hear from her crawled the five that passed after she lifted off.

He'd assembled two teams in that time and herded them all up to the roof. Obstetrician and team, emergency surgical suite on standby. Neonatologist with team and incubator. He saw the wind blowing in the hair flying from the team members, but he didn't hear it. He felt his own clothing ripple and slap at his body, but it felt like watching the drawn-out roil of the canvas on a sailboat. But the air around him sounded dead.

Falling snow muted the air and the sound of beating blades he waited for, hanging his sanity on. His head fell forward and he took a deep breath, clinging to hope like a tangible thing, fists balled and gripping nothing.

Too much snow. It blew hard enough to sting his cheeks, and he immediately flashed to the storm they'd outrun to Schenectady, where she'd had to fight the wind at times, and flown with it at others. But that had been more or less open terrain, not between buildings. If she'd needed to bank to the left or right to work with the wind, she'd had room. She shouldn't be flying in this, not in the city.

"There they are," someone said, and he didn't even know who, just looked at the sky to see the lights of the chopper through the gray gloom.

As she started to descend, a powerful wind gust came from the southwest, blasting the chopper off target toward the building.

His heart stopped dead.

"Are they gonna…?" Someone else said the words he couldn't even bear to think, and all he could do was force frigid air in and out. He closed his eyes.

If she hit the building, he couldn't see it. He couldn't see her die.

The snow deadened the air so much he couldn't even hear the blades beating. It took several painful heartbeats to realize he hadn't heard a crash either, and hadn't heard screams from anyone on the teams he'd assembled.

He opened eyes again, noting that she'd pulled the chopper up and now flew above the buildings, circling again.

He didn't have his radio. He hadn't brought it, not that he could distract her, but as much as he struggled to force himself to watch, he needed to hear her voice. Just to know how she was. Was she freaking out like he was? Was she asking for help?

Out of the corner of his eye he saw the neonatologist's nurse cross herself and bow her head, and he was thankful that someone had the peace of mind to pray.

The chopper began to sink again, but at a much faster speed. He watched, horror again shooting up as quickly as the chopper fell. It looked like she intended on slamming the thing into the roof, but now the sight held him gripped and nothing could make him close his eyes.

Close, closer…

Every muscle in his body strained, his lungs growing so tight he could barely breathe, everything else so tight he shook.

She pulled up just in time to soften the landing, and touched down, with only the smallest bounce at the end. He had to clamp his mouth shut to keep a sob of relief from escaping.

The other doctors took the lead, charging out with the incubator and to fetch the woman on the chopper's gurney. He did the only thing he could. He raced with them to help if needed, but his assistance mainly consisted of helping with a tricky latch that locked the stretcher in place, and once they were out, the lot raced back for the building.

Penny was still shutting down. The motor went quiet and he climbed into the chopper and closed the door behind him.

Alive. She was alive, and all right, and when she looked at him, he took in bright, shining eyes and glowing cheeks. The relief he'd briefly experienced fell to his feet. That was excitement, exhilaration, she hadn't been afraid. He had been afraid. He had been petrified—his insides still shook. But she looked rock solid.

When she stepped out of her seat and walked back to him, even as his hands curled over her shoulders, he didn't know whether he was going to shake her, strangle her, or just grab tight.

As soon as he touched her, the need to be closer

took over and he pulled her with him to fall into the rear seat. His hands found her face, and he kissed her, every aching inch of his heart needing to feel her life, to taste her sweetness, to blot out the past agonizing hours.

Outside, the wind hit them again and rattled the chopper, chilling the already cold vehicle further, but it wasn't going anywhere now. He angled his head and slid his tongue into her mouth, every second touching her, breathing her in, like a balm, reassurance against what the fear still seeping through him still vibrated with: she was going to die.

"Hey." Something made her pull back, and her own small hands on his face made him open his eyes and look at her. "You're shaking. We can go inside. Are you cold? Are you okay?"

The denseness of the question pulled him out of that need to get closer, like the wind rattling the doors, jarring and cold.

"You damned near died." The words croaked out. But saying them once gave him strength, gave him back the anger that had first seized him. The second time, he shouted it. *You damned near died!*

Even shouting, it wasn't enough.

During the hours apart he'd learned what was worse than Nila leaving.

"But I didn't. I'm okay. See? I'm okay." She stroked his face, like she could pet his worry away. The brightness in her eyes dulled a bit, the color faded, like she was just starting to see how horrible the past few hours had been for him.

"You could've died. You had to know how dangerous it was to go. You know better than that. How could you do that?" He pulled her hands from his face, needing her to focus on his words, not soothing him. "How could you put yourself in that much danger?"

The words had no sooner left his mouth than he knew the answer. It didn't matter what she said, this was just how she was. This was what Penny's life was, rolling the dice and always expecting a seven.

She did foolish things, mostly because she wanted to make things better for others, he knew that, had always known that. Even understanding that didn't give him any way to deal with it. All he could do was deal with what was before him right now, and that was a woman who, although he might love her, lived on the edge of disaster.

He put her away from him and climbed out of the chopper, unable to summon any other words. She sat dazed, and he could see her mentally scrambling for the right thing to say, but there was nothing to say.

Penny watched Gabriel climb out of the chopper, senses reeling. The exhilaration of saving a life—of actually knowing this time that she was the one who'd beaten the storm and saved lives, not just luck, faded. She was messing this up with Gabriel. She was messing *them* up.

"I did it because she needed help. If I hadn't gone, she'd have had that baby alone, and probably would have died. They couldn't have ever gotten her back here fast enough."

"Her life is not more valuable than yours. And that baby, that precious baby you helped deliver, is not more precious than our baby."

The wind had rocked her earlier, but Gabriel's words took the wind out of her. And when he slammed the door on the chopper and stalked for the hospital, her chest felt almost caved in from her lack of sufficient breath.

This wasn't going the way she'd pictured. Of course, she'd known he'd be angry, but after she'd—after they'd saved the mother and child, she'd thought he'd calm down. See the earlier small, and admittedly bigger later risk as justified. But when he said it that way...

She scrambled from the back of the chopper to chase him inside. He was getting onto the elevator as she reached him, and she twisted sideways to slip between the doors.

"Wait, please. I'm sorry. It was okay when I went. It was that second line. Snow isn't usually so blustery." She reached for him and he pulled back, shaking his head.

"Don't. I can't do this. I cannot do this again. I can't spend the rest of my life wondering what's the next dangerous, stupid thing you'll do." He swallowed and shook his head. "We can't do this. This isn't going to work."

But he'd kissed her. He'd kissed her the way you kissed someone you loved, or at least felt very deeply for.

"Are you saying you're moving out? You're leaving me?"

"We've never been together. Not really. It was a trial run. Better we learn this early," he said, and the elevator started to go down, and brought a sensation of plummeting in her middle. "I'll move out tonight."

What could she say? There had to be something to say, something that would make it okay for him. "I couldn't let her go through that alone…"

"I told you to go home. I told you to go, you'd have never known."

"You did, but you can't just order me around. If that's your idea of marriage, of a relationship, *that's* why she left."

He flinched, the doors opened, and he walked away again. She didn't even know what floor it was, or where he was aiming. Someone else got on, and she stuck in the corner, unable to bring herself to chase him again.

Go home. Fall apart there. She reached out to press the button for the first floor, but her phone chirruped and she almost lost her mind, fumbling for it, hoping it was him. She wrenched it from her pocket in a heartbeat and looked at the screen.

Text from Charles Davenport. Not Gabriel.

My office.

The new passenger had already pressed the right button, so she slunk back to the corner of the elevator to wait. Like Charles could say anything worse to her than Gabriel had said. If words were teeth, they'd be chewing through her belly, down low where she found her palm pressed and shielding. In that second, she didn't know what to feel worse about.

All the adrenaline she'd been running on was gone, and when the elevator stopped, she had to drag herself out of the back corner and down the hallway to her eldest brother's office. Only he wouldn't be wearing that hat right now, he would be Dr. Charles Davenport, chief of the ER. And she was the pilot who'd violated direct orders.

Charles's secretary waved her through, but the rueful pinch of her mouth said enough. He'd be in a lather, even if it was a Charles special lather, where he'd be too civilized to shove her out of the window even if he really wanted to.

She opened the door to his office and didn't smile, didn't do much of anything except peel her hand away from her womb. She didn't have much emotional currency left to play, but Charles did. He sat behind his desk, hands pressed flat to the desktop, fingers spread out, face red.

Diffusing this situation seemed less important than the situation with Gabriel, so she just held up one hand to signal to him to wait and sat opposite him. Took a breath. Took another. It didn't really help, it gave her oxygen but not words.

As soon as she signaled her readiness, he let loose a stream, echoing the words already seared into her by Gabriel.

Risks. Death. Bad, bad Penny. But it was kind of a blur, right up until the end.

"I asked, do you know what you're doing to the people who love you when you do these things? This isn't new skydiver on a sunny day with a back-up parachute kind of worry, this is watching your sister torment a cobra worry. Do you care that you put your family and friends through that?"

"Yes," she said on reflex, the question so shocked her. Did it really seem like she didn't care about anyone? No other words came. Who knew Charles would be better than Mom with the guilt trip?

Guilt amplified when she remembered the next time she'd see her family. In a few days. At Charles's wedding. These were the last days of work before he married, and things would be stressful enough for him without having to deal with this.

He hadn't even been there to watch her land, or see the wind trying to smash them into the building, but the rant that continued was sharp enough that she'd never have guessed it. It was the end, when he threatened to make funeral arrangements so they'd be prepared, that she just gave up listening and slumped forward in her chair, supporting her head with her palms, elbows on knees.

The day officially crossed over into the territory of Too Much.

"When you have children, maybe you'll understand. Maybe you'll think of family first."

Gabriel's sentiment again, but more pointed. Her direct failure. Her eyes began to well and she could only nod.

He said something about a week-long suspension, and that she'd be fired the next time she violated a no-fly order, like any of that mattered.

Another nod. Her head could move but her mouth could not.

She had to go to Gabriel, that was all she knew, and she stood. She was almost to the door before she realized she probably should ask if he was done. "Am I dismissed?"

He nodded. "Be careful on your way home. The roads are treacherous."

Another nod. She opened the door.

"Pen, I know you went above and beyond for that woman and her baby. I'm proud you have the heart to do things like that. We all need you to be more rational about it."

"I know," she whispered, then, with the tears brimming, she smiled at her brother before leaving. "Thank you."

CHAPTER ELEVEN

PENNY RUSHED THROUGH the door to her apartment and the only lights in the darkened space came from Gabriel's room in the open loft above.

The Christmas lights he'd strung sat dark, no twinkling, and she found herself shaking as she sprinted for the stairs.

After having searched the hospital and called him twice with no answer, Penny had hoped she'd come up with the words to make him stay, but she hadn't. The best she could do was try to explain again, explain better, explain more. Beg.

Up the stairs, she stopped in the doorway of his room and watched him mechanically moving clothing from the bureau to an open duffle bag on the bed.

A greeting would be too flippant.

Running to him to throw her arms around him and beg him to stay would be too much.

"I know I shouldn't have gone," she said, alerting him to her presence. He looked at her, but his eyes were tired. He didn't look like a man hoping to be convinced to stay, but this felt like the most important test of her bravery since she'd taken those first steps after years in a wheelchair.

"I didn't think about our baby," she said, confirming what both Gabriel and Charles had basically said. "I thought about Andrea and how terrified she must've been. How grateful I was to have you here when I was just throwing up. I thought about how hard I would've been praying for you to drop through the ceiling and make everything okay…if that had been me."

He stuffed shirts into his bag and sat, sighing, his voice soft, even gentle compared to his earlier yelling. "I know all this."

"I still needed to say it. And I have to say this too…" But she needed a breath before she fainted from how fast her heart was pounding. "I love you. I'm… I'm in love with you. So hard I can't… I can't be in a parental partnership either. And I can't have a marriage like my parents', all public face and nothing but bitterness and anger inside. No kind of non-relationship with you is going to work for me. If you don't love me, if you don't think you can be with me and make compromises—both of us—to make this life together work, then you're right to leave."

His dark beautiful eyes left her and fixed on the bureau he'd been working from, no words coming. As the seconds ticked and ticked on, she realized no words were going to come.

It wasn't enough.

"My whole life, my thinking was always, 'Can you do this?'" Her voice went wobbly and she felt burning in her eyes again, but she wouldn't get said what she needed to say if she broke down now. A slow breath was all she allowed herself. "For so long the answer was always no. When the answer finally started becoming yes, I just always did it. Whatever I wondered if I could do, if I could, I did. Tonight there was a lull in the snow, and I confirmed it on radar. Then I asked myself, 'Can you make it there?' I knew I could, and it felt like I should help her if I could. I intended to stay there, not fly back. Leave the chopper, ride in the ambulance and return for it once the storm passed. Then she was bleeding and going by ground would've been a death sentence for her. I admit it, I didn't even look at the radar then. I should've, but I didn't because I didn't want to have to make that call for her. I just took the risk. I can't explain it better than that."

She stepped into the room then, pushing every tattered scrap of courage she had left after the day, and rounded the bed to wrap her arms around his bowed head, and curled her head down to rest her cheek on his hair. This might be the last time she ever got to do it, to touch him close. He didn't push her away as he had, but he didn't reach for her either. He didn't put his arms around her to express his own grief at what felt like something dying.

He didn't move, and said nothing…though she wanted to hear his voice so badly she almost begged him to say something. He wanted her gone, that was all she could surmise.

She kissed his head, lovingly, slowly, breathing him in as much as she could, then let go and reached for the duffle he'd just finished filling, zipped it up, and picked it up. "I'll take this downstairs for you."

"Thank you," he said, and it was something. She'd take anything. She'd even have been grateful for yelling, for more words that would ruin her.

At the door, she stopped and looked back at him. One more time. One more attempt. "I felt like half a person back then. Then I got to be whole, and I...guess I got stuck in that new wholeness where I feel free when I'm not tied to the ground. But I'm not just a whole person now, I'm two. I haven't worked out how to do that yet. I've been focused on getting through the pregnancy and the possible health ramifications of my disease. It's a lot to get my head around but I'm trying."

Tears spilled then, and she knew it was going to turn ugly if she didn't get out of there.

"You should wait until the morning to leave. It's awful out there, especially if you're carrying suitcases. In the morning the roads will be better, you'll be able to trust cabbies and not have to lug this all on the subway."

He stood up and for a second she thought maybe he was coming to her, but he bent and pulled a suitcase from under the bed.

Right.

"I'm going to bed. You won't see me. I'll stay out of the way," she said.

She might not be as sensible as everyone wanted,

but she was sensible enough to not stay there and wait for an answer. She hitched the bag higher and immediately carried it downstairs, leaving him to pack and leave, or pack and loiter until morning.

Downstairs, she eyed the bookcase and the albums she'd hidden from him. Words hadn't worked. Maybe pictures. Maybe if he knew what she was struggling against. For all she'd been trying to be open and honest, she'd still kept that part of herself hidden from him, protected this vulnerable spot.

She felt sick, but while he packed, she slipped albums into his duffle, then covered them all up with clothes and zipped it up to put by the sofa.

If he was going to reject her forever, it would be for the whole her, not just the parts she'd let him see.

After Penny's living space, which had been bright and colorful even before he'd strung thousands of twinkling lights, his apartment couldn't compare. It had never felt flat and cold before, but now the neutral colors irritated him. Looked lifeless. Like he couldn't pick a color if he had to. It was supposed to be tasteful, but it was just bland.

He dropped his bags on his brown sofa and sat, using the duffle like an armrest.

He'd stayed until first light, and leaving still didn't feel right. Even after an afternoon in hell, which had hurt even more than when Nila had left. Being the one to leave didn't feel any better.

She'd said love, and he knew it was true just as sharply as he knew it wouldn't work. But he still hated knowing what she was going through too. He'd stayed until morning to keep from giving her worry in return, sitting among the Christmas decorations he'd put up, in a place that now felt more like home to him than his own home.

Over the past two weeks she'd kept hammering about how he didn't trust her, and there couldn't be any question now about whether or not he could trust her to stick around. She might love him, but there would never be stability with her.

He scrubbed his hands over his face and forced himself to get up. Sitting here feeling sorry for himself wouldn't make anything better. He should put up some decorations, try to make his apartment feel like home again. Unpack. Get in some groceries...

Not sit on the couch and mope.

He grabbed the bags and hauled them to his bedroom. Do the things that needed to be done. Keep moving. Don't think about the way she'd kissed his head, hugged it, and he hadn't even put his hands on her in return.

Don't think about how it felt like abandonment and rejection to leave her like that.

He unzipped the duffle and dug his hands into the top layer of shirts, but his knuckles struck something hard. Had he put shoes in there?

Lifting the clothes away, the bottom fell out of his guts. Photo albums sat in his clothes. The albums she'd taken away. Not just taken, the ones she'd hidden behind the others.

His first instinct was to step back from them, ignore them, even put the shirts back and cover them up. A smart man would send them back to her and be done with it.

Hands shaking, he pulled them from the bag. A slip of paper fluttered to the floor.

If this is it, if you're going, I want you to understand. You seeing these still scares me. I'm still working this out. But this fear feels like one of the things that scare me and I should still run toward it.

Strong, hastily scribbled words, devoid of the usual hallmarks of her notes. No smiley faces anywhere either—even if they were her usual method of punctuation. She hadn't even signed it. And he hadn't left her with enough courage to give them to him directly.

Which meant he had to look. She was far from a bad person, and he owed it to her to see what she now wanted him to see. Even if it couldn't change anything. She was like lightning across a dark sky, beautiful to watch but scarring or deadly if you got too close.

Tucking them under his arm, he headed for the living room, stopping at the fridge to get a beer.

Blue album: *Penny's Birthdays.*

Red album: *Penny's Progress.*

Progress? A strangely detached way to chronicle your child's life…

He opened the blue album. It started with the first birthday. His first time seeing baby Penny. She was all eyes, those dazzling blue eyes, and smiles. Ribbons in her baby curls. Pushing a bear-themed walker around and honking the horn while laughing. People in the background winced.

He felt a small smile. How much would their child look like her? Would his dark brown eyes overwhelm those dazzling blues? His mother had hazel eyes, and her father's eyes had been green. There was a chance for blue.

Two. Favorite gift, tiny tricycle. No horn, had a bell this time. Chubby toddler legs. Bunnies to pet or chase while laughing, if that picture was anything to go by. Then half-naked and running from Mom, cake and frosting covering her face and mashing her hair up at an insane angle on one side.

He couldn't help his smile then. That was his girl. Half-naked, running around laughing, covered in cake.

The smile faltered. Was his. Not is.

Three. Small trampoline with safety bars. Pigtails. Skinned knee. Always running.

When had she started to get ill? He felt it lurking, like some hulking monster, ready to take away those rosy cheeks.

He sped through four, through five, six... More of the same, happy, bright, lively.

Seven. The seventh birthday was different. Indoors. At a table. Dressed in ruffles and ribbons. An angry red rash cascaded down her right cheek, around her eyes. Her swollen eyes. So red on her pale skin. She sat behind a cake burning seven candles but didn't smile for the camera.

Other pictures followed, showing her opening gifts. He could see the rash on her knuckles and marked the ones that had cracked to bleed by the bandages covering them.

Then a picture of a box someone else had to open. Too heavy, he realized, or she'd simply grown too tired. It was a disease that sapped strength. Mom posed for the picture that followed, showing the gift. Telescope.

The gifts on the first six birthdays had been the kind to encourage play, physical toys. But this toy was sedate for the little girl who'd been so active.

His chest burned sharper but hadn't really stopped since yesterday.

He put the book down and leaned back, just to get his breath. And to guzzle his beer. To remind himself that she'd gotten better. She was better now.

But when had she gotten better?

Dropping the empty bottle on the table, he picked up the album again and flipped the page.

Eight. Birthday in a pool. Water wings on her arms and Mom behind her, holding her for safety. Scrawny little body.

Nine. On the back of a pony with Dad holding her.

Ten. In a wheelchair.

No smiles. No smiles anymore. Never smiles. It was like looking at the embodiment of suffering. Her family loved her and the weaker she got the closer they held her, but her eyes were just dead. None of that Penny spark shone there.

He put the birthday album back down and reached for the other. He'd spent a half hour watching her deteriorate. He needed to see some progress.

But that's not what it showed. The first fifteen or so sheets of images showed progression, not progress. Small, fragile, but trying so hard to do what the therapists told her. Tears. So many tears.

God, this wasn't any better.

He skipped chunks he simply couldn't bear to see, and didn't stop turning pages until he saw a twelve-or thirteen-year-old Penny in a safety harness, gripping parallel bars and walking. Supported, but walking. And smiling. With no fresh redness on her face, just a lingering pink shadow of it around her eyes, those brilliant, shining, hope-filled blue eyes.

Progression became progress. She worked the bars, bearing more weight in every picture as her cheeks and arms filled out.

She used weight machines, and her legs grew thicker, took on definition. Grew strong.

Braces became crutches, became a cane, became nothing. And her smile, God, her smile...

My whole life, my thinking was always, "Can you do this?" And for so long the answer was always no. When the answer finally started becoming yes, I just always did it.

He picked up the first album and flipped to those teenaged birthday parties.

Thirteen. Go-karts.

Fourteen. Horseback riding without someone holding her.

Fifteen. He couldn't tell what was going on, just that there were girls and boys in bathing suits, running amok in the surf at the beach, and probably some kind of wet sand fight? There was sand flinging, which wasn't entirely safe without protective eyewear...

Sixteen. Dancing with friends and live music in the background. Who knew where…?

Always outside. So happy. So alive.

They'd had to hold her up, and then it became holding her back from all the things she wanted to do, and she'd pushed back against it. She hadn't sought out dangerous things because of some kind of desire for an adrenaline high, she'd wanted to do things that celebrated that freedom she'd fought so hard for. And to help others who were hurting. She understood suffering.

He didn't want to be someone who held her back. He wanted to celebrate with her, to see that sparkle in her eyes.

The sparkle that hadn't been there last night.

She'd gotten used to fighting for her freedom, and he'd gotten used to protecting himself. It couched all his decisions—that need to be safe.

Until that night…

CHAPTER TWELVE

PENNY CHECKED THE GPS as she turned down
the drive where it told her, into trees, somewhere
on the outskirts of Gabriel's hometown in New
Jersey.

She hadn't heard from him the day he'd left,
hadn't seen him that morning. She'd promised to
stay out of his way and she had.

But she *had* heard the moment he'd gone, and
even if she hadn't heard the door closing, she
still would've known. A whole night awake fantasizing that he'd find her albums and change
his mind had made her even more hypersensi-
tive to his presence than usual. The moment he'd
stepped out, all the hope had left her, had left
with him.

Then she'd cried.

The next day had passed the same way—not
knowing if he'd found them, if they'd made any
difference. If he'd cared. If he even still wanted

to be part of their child's life or if she'd ruined that too.

By the time his text had come late last night— We need to talk—along with some coordinates and a time, her hopes had fallen too far to even speculate about his thoughts.

On the drive, she'd conjured two options: meet his parents because he did still want the baby. Or meet at a lawyer's office because he did still want the baby, as in sole custody.

The long, private drive said *parents*. Which was good. She'd take it—she'd take whatever she could get.

Through the thick line of trees running along the drive she saw a field of white, and then color. Red and white checks like a massive gingham picnic blanket.

And then the trees opened out and she saw a big gingham hot-air balloon.

Her heart stuttered.

She sped up to get to the end of the road, wherever the heck it was, and around the bend came to a parking area before a massive red horse barn. Gabriel was there, leaning against the front fender of his car, arms crossed, knit cap and coat to warm him in the frosty but bright, sunny day.

She parked right beside him and got out, going a bit snow blind with the early afternoon rays bouncing off the snow. Snatching her glasses, she put them on and closed the car door.

The hot-air balloon could just be there by some coincidence. Maybe. She was afraid to get her hopes up or even to look at him, though the glasses made it a little easier as she could hide it if she got weepy again.

He didn't say anything but she could feel him watching as she pulled her gloves on and went to lean on his car beside him.

"Is that balloon for you?"

"Yes."

"I thought they only flew them when it was warm?"

"They usually do," he said softly, "but I begged."

Pregnancy-safe adventure. They'd even talked about this as a possibility. Oh, her hopes, they were climbing.

"It's not dangerous?"

"It's cold. People don't do it because it's very cold." His arms uncrossed and he slid one down her arm to take her gloved hand in his own. "Want to try it?"

She nodded, smiling even as she felt sneaky tears trying to leak out and had to dip her free hand up to swipe under her glasses before he saw them. "Even if you planned on chucking me out of the basket at ten thousand feet."

"You know better than that," he said softly, but let go of her hand and rounded to the trunk of his car. He soon returned with the largest parka she'd ever seen, and a thick, wooly beanie too. He pulled the hat onto her head, mashing her hair down, and she didn't care at all.

Standing so close and not touching him when her arms ached to wrap around him took strength of will she'd have doubted she possessed, but this felt like something that had to happen at his pace. The man liked to take his time in things…

"You only brought one big coat? That's not going to fit either of us." She tilted her head back so he could adjust her hat, and closed her eyes against the blinding afternoon sun.

"Trust me, I have a plan," he said, then, with her eyes to the sun, face lifted, she felt the brush of something cold and firm on her lips. It took a second, but she identified it.

Lip balm.

He did have a plan. Keep her warm, protect her lips from the wind. She smiled.

"Perfect. That makes it easier," he said, and finished. Then, before she could open her eyes, he pressed his lips to her newly moisturized mouth.

It was probably supposed to be a sweet little smooch, but the second she felt his warm lips against hers, her restraint evaporated. All the hurt of the past—Lord, she'd lost count how many days, it felt like years—evaporated with it.

This time, when her arms whipped around his shoulders, his came around her too, and he didn't kiss her back in the way of a man suffering her touch or indifferent to it. He angled his head, held her tighter, kissed deeper, until it was clumsy and wet, teeth, tongues, tears, and skewed sunglasses.

"This isn't the plan, baby." He panted more than spoke, his lips brushing hers with every syllable. Then lifted his head and pulled the glove off one hand so he could wipe the tears on her cheeks. "These will freeze up there."

She sniffed, then laughed a little and eased her hands back down. "I think I need more lip balm…"

He presented the tube, winked, and while she reapplied it, he put on the massive parka.

"Doors locked?"

She stuck the balm into her pocket, pulled out her key fob, and locked the door. With the keys stashed again, and her hands back in gloves, he put his arm around her waist and led, their steps crunching across the snowy field.

Two people waited at the balloon—the captain she could identify because he climbed into the basket, and a man at the moorings to knock off the anchor ropes when they were ready.

She didn't know how high they were going to go, but they couldn't reach her hopes and the burst of joy that had her just a little terrified she was getting too far ahead of herself.

The prospect of how much colder she knew it would be even a few hundred feet off the ground should probably factor into that fear, but it didn't. Gabriel would always try to keep her and the baby safe, and he was too sensible to go up for any other reason but to show her something. He loved her. He had to.

"Think you have room in there for me to huddle in? I'm not sure my wool coat is going to be warm enough. Also, I'm hoping to force you to hug me for a long stretch of time. It's my clever plan that I'm telling you like the villain at the end of a movie when they think they have the hero in the right place and…" She stopped, chuckling at herself. "Those thoughts started out from a much funnier place than they became as I kept explaining."

"They didn't have any parkas in your size, so I got the big one to share. It was my plan all along. My improvised romantic plan when they didn't have your size."

She smiled then and stepped in front of him, pressed her back to his front, and clamped her arms at her sides to keep them out of the way.

"Sleeves."

"Really?" She looked at the sleeves and then back at him. "Are you going to have one and me the other?"

"We could do that, but you'll probably be warmer if my arm is there too. The sleeves are big."

Penny wasn't about to put up a fuss about anything. She eyed the sleeves to make sure they were roomy enough, then just shrugged and went with it. It'd be better if her coat were off so she could actually feel him without the layers between them, but maybe that would come later. He had said *romantic*.

When it was done, and only her fingertips poked out of the wrists, making her hands utterly useless, he stiffly zipped them in. He was right, it was warm, and nice with him behind her, around her. To smell him, even among all this new-coat smell. Made the hard days blur about the edges.

Below, the land fell away as they rose. Gabriel lifted their arms together so he could pull up the hood, then rested his chin on her shoulder so they were both protected from the wind.

"How did you set this up so fast? Or did you do it when we talked about it?"

"I did it yesterday. Their schedule was totally open," he said, and then added in a softer voice, "It was easier to arrange than the mental stuff."

"The not wanting to be anywhere near me bit?"

"That wasn't it. It was more being afraid to be with you." His mouth stayed at her ear, making it easy to hear over the wind. "Actually, that's not it. You kept saying I didn't trust you, and you were right. After Nila left, I always held part of myself back, and when I realized what you and the baby mean to me, I was in some broken pattern of trying to protect you both, or trying to protect myself. You humbled me. I know what it took for you to show me those albums, the albums that almost killed me."

She closed her eyes and let those words wash over her. Then turned her head toward him so the crosswinds wouldn't eat her words. "It was easier than you think, when it became necessary. If you were going to leave me, I wanted you to leave the real me. I should've let you see them before."

"You were protecting yourself. I get it. Neither of us were ready. If I'd looked then, I might not have seen it. Especially after having just looked at your Adventure album."

"Seen what?"

"What really drives you."

She hadn't really ever thought about her motivators aside from the excitement of *doing stuff.* "What do you think drives me?"

"Life. You just want to experience what life has to offer. You don't do things that people frequently die doing. You use safety equipment. You always buckle in when you fly. You don't *chase* death. You chase experiences," he explained, shaking his head. "Did you just want me to say it, or do you not really know this?"

She shrugged He'd feel her shoulders creep up his chest, and no doubt saw her brows moving her knit cap.

"You told me you need *adventures*. That was your word, so on some level you know your motives. You didn't say you wanted thrills, stunts, or even fun. You said adventure."

"Yeah, okay. I guess that's right." She straightened and looked out over the sea, only realizing then that they were drifting out over the bay to the Atlantic. The gray winter water below still sparkled under the sun, and toward the northwest she could see the city skyline in the distance.

"I want to have adventures with you. I don't want to watch and worry. If you storm the gates of hell, I need to be storming them with you."

She smiled, and even her lip balm felt like it was stiffening from the cold, but she didn't want to cut their time short. "I promise not to storm the gates of hell. Or exclude you."

"I promise to work every day not to hold back from you, even if you're the one person in the world with the power to destroy me."

His words bounced around in her heart and she tried to turn to him, but her arms were stuffed in the sleeves and he'd wrapped their arms around her, which made it impossible. "I wouldn't... I wouldn't ever destroy you."

"I know. In my heart I know you would never do anything to hurt me, not on purpose. Logically, I know that it's going to be a struggle, me wanting to hold back. But you have a way of breaking through those barriers. I need that." He held her gaze as she twisted as best she could to look at him. "I need you. I asked you to marry me, and I told myself it was just for the well-being of the baby, but I need you. And I can give you however long you need, as long as you keep fighting for me too."

Her lower lip quivered and her throat had closed up again, so she nodded with as much vigor as she could manage tucked against him like that.

"Do you know the best adventure for us?"

She did. Oh, she did. But she needed to hear

him say it, even if it would just be whispered in her ear.

"A life together. Laughing, fighting, driving each other crazy, knocking over Christmas trees because we can't stop touching long enough to lie down sensibly." He said the words she'd been waiting for. "Never giving up on one another. Raising our kids. Going on vacations to…scuba dive in the Keys or…to Iceland for the Northern Lights…"

It all sounded perfect, even before he said the thing that was sure to rip her guts out.

"Doing with them all the things Penelope didn't get to do."

Tears on her cheeks would freeze so she turned her head to him so he could see her cheeks. He was the one mostly in control of their hands right now.

"None of that," he said, reaching up to rub them away with his gloved hand, and then brought their arms together so he could cuff the left sleeve enough to expose her hand. Then took off her glove.

She started to pull the shared-sleeve arm to

her face to get to her cheeks, but he already had them bending down and in.

"Pocket," he said.

She slipped her hand into the pocket, confused. Pockets were warm…

Except this one had a small velvet box in it.

"No balling my fist up for warmth with this thing in there," she said, closing her fingers over the box, and they pulled it from the pocket in tandem.

Gabriel stuffed her glove into the other pocket, then removed his own on the right, and stashed it too. Right hand his, left hand hers, he reached for the box. "Hold tight."

She nodded, and watched as he raised the lid. A glittering diamond winked at her from the black interior. "Man, I never thought I'd be excited to get an engagement ring, but if you don't hurry up I'm gonna die."

She'd have to tell him later that she didn't need a long engagement. He'd gone to such lengths to plan this, and he'd said even more than her heart had been aching to hear for what felt like years.

He plucked the ring from the velvet perch and she flipped her hand over to flex her fingers out to receive it. And dropped the box right over the edge, into the sea.

"Oh, no... Oh, *no*! You got it? You got it, right?" she babbled, until he showed it to her. "Hurry, before we drop it too! Hot-air balloons are dangerous if you've got butter fingers. Maybe we should step back from the edge of the basket."

In answer, he slipped the ring onto her finger.

"You know, in my head, I was going to kiss the ring, it was going to be extremely romantic. But now I'm thinking gloves."

"Yes. Yes, gloves." She laughed, and between the two of them wrestled her left glove on over the ring, and his right one back on.

As soon as the maneuver was complete, Penny wiggled and turned, pulling her arms from the sleeves.

"Pen?" Despite his confusion, he held still, didn't try to stop her.

She didn't stop, even to explain, until she'd gotten her arms free and spun inside the oversized coat to get her arms around him.

His smile was beautiful, and short-lived. She tugged on him and leaned up on her toes, mouth presented for kissing. That was all it took to convince him to kiss her again. Kiss for real. Kiss enough to make the balloon captain feel awkward, probably.

When he lifted his head, she felt words bubbling out. "When you said to meet you in New Jersey, I joked to Miranda in my best mafia talk, 'He's gonna make me an offer I can't refuse.' But I really thought maybe you wanted me to meet your parents, or maybe you'd told them about me and they wanted to meet me and asked. But you really did ask me to New Jersey to make me an offer I couldn't refuse."

"I did." He laughed again, "But that's not New Jersey. *The Godfather* was set in New York."

"It was?"

He nodded.

"I've never watched it. I only know that line. I just thought it was Jersey, for some reason."

"You never watched *The Godfather*?"

She shook her head again and teased, "Is the wedding off now?"

His disapproving squint was beautiful, and full of charm. "No. It just means we have to watch some movies before we get married. Or on our honeymoon. However, to answer your other question, my parents do want to meet you. Just not today. I want you to myself today."

"Me too. Let's go home."

"You're done with the balloon flight adventure?"

"It's cold," she whispered, then gave him her best sexy eyebrow wiggle over the top of her glasses. "I have another adventure in mind."

"Do you?"

"Mmm-hmm. A sexy adventure. Then a nap."

There her stomach pitted a little and she knew she lost the flirty glint in her eyes, but still kept looking over the top edge so he could see her. "And you stay. You're there…"

"When you wake up?"

She nodded.

"I can guarantee it."

"Even if you need to go to the bathroom."

"Is that a question?"

"No. I mean I need you to be there when I wake up, so wake me up first. Or put a sign on the pillow that says 'Be Right Back.'"

"We might need to talk about this later."

"*Humor* me."

"We'll have a neon sign made up, and I'll flip

the switch so that it says: 'Gabriel has Gone to the Bathroom. Don't Go Looking for Him.'"

Satisfied, she nodded, grinning and raising her face for another kiss. But he took her cheeks in both hands and pushed the brim of her hat up with his thumbs to bare the space between her brows, then pressed his lips to her forehead and lingered there. A feeling she could only call relief started where his lips touched her head and then seeped into the rest of her body, down to her toes. The need for hungry kisses faded back for the moment, and as the soft, loving kiss faded, she rested her cheek against his shoulder and let that sweetness fill her.

They stayed like that a long time, paying no attention to the views or the cold. It was the lump on her left ring finger stretching her gloves tight that made her think about weddings. "Oh—ah— are you going to be my date tomorrow?"

"You can assume I'm going to be your date for everything."

His words made her smile, and she had to drag herself away from drifting right back into that happy place again. "Charles's wedding... I don't think we should tell the family about our engagement or the baby tomorrow. It's their special day and I don't want to stomp all over it. So I'll need you to put the ring back on me tomorrow when we get home."

"And not mention the suspension?"

Oh, yeah, the suspension. And her father, Chief of the ER before Charles had ascended to his position. "Yeah, let's leave that out too. I don't want to…make a scene when Dad decides to drown me in the chocolate fountain."

He laughed and made all the right sounds of agreement, then directed her to look toward the other side of the balloon, at the skyline in the distance.

The captain had turned them back toward land. Bless him.

"I think we owe him a good tip," she murmured against his neck.

"A better tip than 'Don't take lovestruck idiots up in the middle of winter'?"

"I'm pretty sure he's got that one already."

EPILOGUE

Seven months later...

THE CAB PULLED up outside the emergency doors of Manhattan Mercy, and Gabriel breathed a sigh of relief to see his brother-in-law, Zac, waiting there with a wheelchair.

In the backseat beside him, Penny held his hand but said nothing. She'd taken up meditation as a way to get through the last few months of pregnancy, when she truly had felt restricted, and now sat with her eyes closed, practicing deep, mindful breathing. It might not be Lamaze exactly, but whatever worked for her, he was happy to support. Especially since one of them needed to be calm for this, and he'd passed calm ten blocks back.

The hold she had on his hand tightened, clueing him in on the approaching contraction. She squeezed hard enough that he could feel her racing heart.

"We're here," he said gently, then opened the door with his free hand.

She opened her eyes to the sight of Zac rolling the wheelchair toward the cab, and her heart rate kicked up higher. "Who does he think is sitting in that?"

No sooner had the words flown than the contraction crested and she squeezed his hand hard enough to pop his knuckles. He sat with her, waiting, breathing, for it to pass. "It's just until we get upstairs."

"I can walk," she panted, then nudged him so that he took the hint and got out. A short time later he had her out and paid the cabbie, but when he turned back, he found her arguing with Zac about the chair.

"You're in labor."

"I figured that out when it was my womb that started seizing up."

"You know hospital policy."

"I don't care about hospital policy. Let's just walk in quickly. You can roll behind us and if I have to sit down, if another one comes...before we get upstairs...we'll cross that bridge..." Obviously it was his turn to be the calmer one. Luckily, he'd planned for this.

He took her hand again and didn't even attempt to drag her the remaining two feet to the chair. Wheelchairs were emotional landmines for Penny. Before they'd decided it was time to come to the hospital, she'd even suggested they should call an ambulance when they still had time, because gurneys were better than wheelchairs.

He sat in the chair, then gestured to his lap with his free hand. "I'm sitting in the chair, you're sitting on me."

It stopped the argument, and when she looked at him, he saw her eyes soften, and she even smiled.

"That's against policy too," Zac said, but his heart didn't sound in it.

"I don't care about hospital policy." This time the words came out of Gabriel's mouth. He simply locked the wheels, then helped ease his waddling wife onto his lap. When they were settled, he unlocked the wheels.

Zac's lip service to policy became evident when he fell in behind them and began pushing them toward the sliding double doors and into the hospital.

* * *

Nearly twelve hours later, in the middle of the night, Mia Jackson came into the world. Penny handled birth far better than she had handled the last month of pregnancy, when she'd repeatedly insisted she was so large, the baby had invited over friends to have a "pool party" in her womb.

Now, as Gabriel sat by his sleeping wife, holding his baby girl, throat so full of happiness and gratitude, he half feared he'd drown on the thick, syrupy sweetness filling him if he breathed too deeply. And he couldn't take his eyes off the little sleeping face, or the tiny hand wrapped around his fingertip.

"Penny for your thoughts."

He smiled at his wife's sleepy, quiet, exhausted voice.

"Penny's always in my thoughts," he whispered, not wanting to wake Mia as she'd had just as hard a day. Catching sight of Penny over the head of their sleeping newborn, he asked, "How are you feeling?"

"Tired. Sore. *Wonderful*," she said. Then she added, "You didn't answer."

He didn't answer because his heart was too

full to translate any of it into words. Instead, he handled what was before him. "Do you want to hold her?"

In answer, and with the help of the bed controls, she sat up and held her arms out. "Still not what you were thinking."

Slowly, he rose and transferred the warm little bundle into her arms, then stood back to take them both in. Penny had held Mia briefly right after she'd been cleaned up, but a long labor had left her too exhausted to really *meet* their daughter before. The grin that split her face flashed like a tropical sunrise, and he knew what she was smiling at before she lifted a hand to stroke through the fullest head of downy black hair he'd ever seen on such a tiny baby.

"I was thinking how much she looks like Baby Penny, but with more enviable locks." He murmured one of a thousand wondrous thoughts that had filled his mind the past few hours.

With soft laugh and the misty eyes, she nodded, clearly as overcome as he'd spent the hours being.

"And that we're going to teach her to crawl, to walk, and to run. And how to know what things she should always run toward."

The family motto, and they still occasionally debated the list of *things*.

A tear fell onto one tiny hand, and she smoothed it away just as he reached out to do the same to her cheeks. "Think we'll have it figured out by the time she's running?" she asked.

He knew her way of loving teasing, always sunshine on his days. "We have a good start on it. Always run toward us. That should buy us some time."

"Always run toward each other," she said, lifting her eyes again to him, and that playful light he loved had been replaced by such devoted reverence he almost lost it. It was a promise, one she silently made every day.

Once again speech left him. All he could do was nod, his life so full of goodness and beauty he couldn't believe it, but knew he'd never let it go.

"Hey."

He looked up again.

She slowly shifted to the side to make room in her bed, and looked down at the space she'd made.

"What about hospital policy?"

"I don't care about hospital policy," she dutifully murmured.

Moments later, he reclined with her, holding his whole family in his arms. As they looked down at her, Mia quietly opened her eyes.

"They're blue," Penny whispered.

Gabriel kissed her temple. "I told you they would be."

* * * * *

LET'S TALK
Romance

For exclusive extracts, competitions
and special offers, find us online:

f facebook.com/millsandboon

📷 @millsandboonuk

🐦 @millsandboon

Or get in touch on 0844 844 1351*

For all the latest titles coming soon,
visit millsandboon.co.uk/nextmonth